THE MYTHMASTER

She was wandering aimlessly down the steps of the building, her eyes focused on distant lands, her pale hands folded in front of her like those of a polite schoolgirl who knows the teacher is looking.

The man approached her. He released the trigger of his glowgas gun and left a harmless identifying mark on the girl's forehead. It would disappear in time. And she might never know that she had been violated. His victims often did not realise that they were pregnant. These unknowing ones were lucky. Because they had not learned that they had a child to lose — and had lost it to the Mythmaster.

He was a pirate of the lowest sort — he stole human lives. And the most powerful criminal in the starlanes wanted to own him — and the woman he hated.

Mythmaster

Leo P. Kelley

CORONET BOOKS
Hodder Fawcett Ltd., London

Copyright © 1973 by Leo P. Kelley

First published 1973 by Dell Publishing Co., Inc,
New York

Coronet edition 1974

Printed and bound in Great Britain for Coronet Books,
Hodder Fawcett Ltd., St. Paul's House, Warwick Lane,
London, EC4P 4AH by Cox & Wyman Ltd, London, Reading
and Fakenham

ISBN 0 340 18832 4

CHAPTER ONE

His name was John Shannon.

On his face was a white-welted scar that slid from the corner of his right eye down the sloping path of his cheek to curve under his lower lip and give it an odd, angular lift. And when he walked, he limped, listing to the left a little, like a ship carrying unevenly distributed cargo.

As he stood at the control panel of his ship, the orders he gave were familiar to his crew, and welcome.

'Release the pellets,' he said.

At once the hundreds of spherical pellets began to drop down upon the North New England minimegalopolis far below the hovering ship. The pellets were black, an ominous rain.

'Prepare to attack,' he commanded. 'Ready the pods for landing.'

In other parts of the ship, crewmen touched buttons or flicked switches, obedient and efficient. The ship drifted down as if in search of the pellets that had just been released from it.

Shannon studied the sensors on the control panel before him. A needle quivered behind a barrier of glass and began to ascend a curved numerality that told its own esoteric story. Shannon's face was expressionless. When the needle reached 100, he spoke again into the ship's communication system. 'Rawley,' he said to the biologist, 'we're going down. I want as many as possible this time. Maxevitch, you and Devlin will move fast. Last time, you acted like we were on some kind of picnic. Well, this is business. The Mythmadness down there now is at Point Prime. Board the pods. *Move!*'

In the corridors of the ship, crewmen moved swiftly aboard

the pods. Those who would remain behind to secure the ship during the bizarre battle about to begin below took up their stations.

Four pods dropped out of the belly of the ship. As they descended into the rising mist of the hallucinogen that had been contained in the dropped pellets, they extended their legs like languid insects aroused by spring.

Shannon, in the first of the four pods, chose his landing place – the rooftop of a huge apartment complex – with the care and the practised eye of a man long familiar with such operations.

'Starson,' he said, addressing his young astrogator, who stood beside him. 'Mark the pregnant ones with glowgas as usual, and let's keep them together as much as possible. We don't want to go searching all over hell's half-acre for them like last time. It cuts down on our lead time and gives the Patrol time to zero in on us. You ready?'

'I'm ready. Only . . .'

'Only what?'

'Maxevitch monitored an ultrafrequency message this morning. It was from Oxon Kaedler's ship. He's offering a reward for information that will put him on our trail.'

'Kaedler doesn't concern me. Does he worry you?'

'He's determined to take over your smuggling operation. Not that he needs it. He's richer than Croesus times ten. He's also dangerous now that he's dead – *legally* dead, at least. The Patrol can't arrest him, and the courts can't prosecute him. Kaedler strikes me as a man worth worrying about.'

'The door of my ship is always open. If Kaedler worries you, you can walk out as easily as you walked in. At any time. But now, man your station.'

Starson turned a dial, and the legs of the pod touched the top of the building. The shock was brief and shallow, nothing more than a tremor. 'We're down, Shannon. Shall I tell them that the Mythmaster has come calling?'

Shannon was feeling the thrill of absolute power that always surged through him at such moments. There was no need, he knew, for Starson to announce the presence of the

Mythmaster. The people outside the ship in the contaminated area already had learned of it; of that he had no doubt. They were already performing their frenzied and unwilling welcome for the Mythmaster, who held them all temporarily in thrall and whose exploits would headline the next teledition of the Fastfax. The journalistic vultures who wrote heated copy for the insatiable Fastfax had long ago dubbed Shannon 'Mythmaster'. The name appealed to them and to their starved readers, who were not interested in bland statistics concerning spacelane deaths on holidays or gutless reports of the latest miniwar in some distant part of Earth or on one of her planetary colonies. No, they wanted to read about murder, for example; and the bloodier, the better. They wanted to sate themselves on gore: CHILD TORN TO BITS BY WILD BEASTS ON MAYCLIFF MOOR! Later today, they'd be delighted to read about the latest attack of the infamous Mythmaster.

Starson had the pod's door down and was standing beside it. The mist of Mythmadness began to swirl into the interior of the pod. Shannon quickly swallowed an antidote capsule, as did the rest of the crewmen, before striding down the graded steps cut into the inner surface of the door.

He and Starson went down together through the building. They burst into apartments, where they found people singing or screaming or moaning, all of them lost in exotic worlds that the hallucinogenic pellets had released upon them from the darkness inside their own skulls.

Starson moved swiftly past the people frantically crowding the corridors. He carried the tiny control box which would identify the particular women he was seeking. Its sensitive needle, he saw, now indicated the nearness of the right kind of woman.

She was wandering aimlessly down the steps of the building, her eyes focused on distant lands, her pale hands folded in front of her like those of a polite schoolgirl who knows the teacher is looking.

Starson approached her. He released the trigger of his glowgas gun, and a purple blast shot out from it and left a harmless identifying mark on the girl's forehead. It would disappear in time. And she might never know that she had been violated, because, as was frequently the case, the Mythmaster's victims did not realise that they were pregnant. These unknowing ones were lucky. Because they had not learned that they had a child to lose – and had lost it to the Mythmaster. No message concerning their fruited state had yet reached their brain from the mysterious canals of their flesh.

Starson unlocked the girl's hands and dragged her along behind him as he bounded down the remaining steps. On the way, he marked an older woman who was cowering in a corner on the building's lowest landing. He whistled a signal to Shannon. Shannon spotted the woman, came down and pulled her to her feet, and sent her careening down the steps, a planet of flesh about to be plundered.

Outside on the streets — carnival!

People milled about, all distraught jesters in a strange court where the King's name was unknown and he ruled with the wildness of chaos. Automobiles had collided with one another. The body of a man from which life had fled in horror lay beneath the left-front wheel of a truck tilted against a leaning lamp-post. Five people — three men and two women — danced merrily down the streets in a circle, their hands linked and their heads thrown back in a delirium of delight that would pass when the effects of the hallucinogen had dissipated, leaving them alone and wondering what odd road they had been travelling, and with whom. And why.

Lee Rawley came running down the street.

'Yo!' Starson yelled. He pointed to the two glowgassed women.

Rawley's hand and the hypodermic it held touched both the woman and the girl, and they crumpled at his feet, unconscious. He knelt first beside the girl. He cut away a portion of her clothes. He made the necessary incision. Staring through the microscopic lenses he had placed in contact with the pupils of his eyes, he located and extracted the fertilised egg that was not yet an embryo from the body of the

8

helpless girl. He placed it in the container hanging from his belt, where it rolled invisibly in a minus-forty-degree solution. He sprayed the wounds his scalpel had left on the girl's abdomen. The flesh promptly fused. Not even a scar would remain to bear witness to his once-upon-a-dark-time predatory presence.

While he performed the same smooth, swift operation on the older woman, the girl regained consciousness and rose to her feet slowly, a lovely flower opening to the summons of the summer sun. The glowgas insignia had already begun to fade from her forehead. Now it was a faintly bluish tinge resembling a cluster of tender veins beneath her skin.

'Oh, come and dance with me!' she cried, holding out her hands to Rawley, who was still kneeling over the other woman.

Shannon appeared suddenly and shoved the girl, sending her sprawling. 'Go!'

She got up and went, shaking her head in bewilderment. It was clear from the expression on her young face that she did not like this man who had hurt her and whose own face was so hard and unconcerned.

Rawley rose and followed Starson's track, which was marked by a ragged line of glowgassed women. He functioned fast and well.

Shannon checked on Maxevitch and Devlin. He discovered that they had located more than a score of women and had locked them all behind the iron fence of a tiny park set in the centre of a traffic circle. Shannon scanned the sky. The Patrol ships would be arriving soon, as soon as it was learned that communication with the area had been substantially reduced. Suspicion would give rise to prompt investigation.

While he was watching the progress of his men and mentally calculating the rewards for all of them symbolised by the small bottles hanging from Rawley's belt, the first of the Patrol ships appeared in the sky. They wove in and out of the rising mist of Mythmadness like frustrated fish in unpredictable ocean currents. No matter. They would not descend and submit to Mythmadness. Shannon laughed. Perhaps the

9

day would come when the Patrol would discover the chemical constituency of his pellets, and then it would be only a matter of time until they would learn how to construct the antidote. But by then he would be in another business, hopefully one even more lucrative than stealing fertilised eggs from the helpless bodies of anaesthetised woman and later selling them to the highest bidder, unconcerned as to what use the buyer would ultimately put the human beings that would develop from those eggs.

Shannon, watching the efficient and rapid progress of his crewmen at their tasks, sent his laughter soaring again into the sky that was quickly filling with Patrol ships.

The men ranged out in orderly fashion. Starson located and identified each pregnant woman with a burst of glowgas. Maxevitch, Devlin, and several other crewmen herded the women into caches of fleshly treasure. Rawley and his companions performed their brief operations. They were a team, a machine, a marvellously effective, almost robotised entity, each functioning as an individual with his own particular task, and all co-operating skilfully to achieve their mutual goal.

While the Patrol ships circled overhead, afraid to fire and risk wounding or killing the victims instead of the victimisers, the crew's work progressed smoothly until each woman within a half-mile radius of the apartment building that was their operational base had been either ignored because she was infertile or left bereft of the life she had begun to nourish. A few pregnant women were allowed to remain pregnant, not out of kindness or consideration by the Mythmaster's crewmen, but because investigation revealed that their embryos were too far developed for transportation in the unique way Shannon employed.

Shannon gave the signal over his communicator that linked him to his far-ranging colleagues. When they had all returned, incongruously sober in the Mythmad milieu through which they moved, he raised his hand, shouted orders, and they boarded the four pods for the ascent to the mother ship.

The only really dangerous part of the mission now faced them. They would have to break through the overhead net of Patrol ships. The force fields they activated to shield the pods would be their major protection, but the fields were not entirely failsafe. The Patrol had recently learned that a steady barrage of missiles directed at a single point on the field could partially penetrate, and, although not totally destroy the pod being attacked, could disable it sufficiently to make capture probable. The Patrol had learned that the missiles were effective almost by accident, a month ago, when one of their launchers had jammed and several bursts of missiles had hit in one spot and downed one of the pods. Shannon had lost two valuable crew members, a pod, and not a little of his towering pride during the mêlée.

Now, as the pods lifted from the building where they had been moored, Shannon gave instructions to his men on each pod. They were to take a circuitous route through the skies and the skein of Patrol ships. Pod One – Shannon's – would emerge first from the cover of the Mythmist and function as a decoy. When most of the Patrollers were in pursuit of Pod One, the other three could make it safely back to the ship. Shannon would then make a run for it. He asked for confirmation from each of the pods and got it.

He broke through into bright sunlight and veered sharply to the left, then up several hundred feet, down a few, and then off to the right. The Patrol ships sped like bees to the hive after him. The irregular path his pod took made a concentrated, focused missile attack impossible.

'Where are they?' Shannon yelled to Starson, referring to the other three pods.

Starson studied the blips on the screen set into the pod's control panel and reported, 'They're almost there. One's made it!' He fell silent, watching the screen intently. 'So have the other two. We can head home now.'

The hive suddenly deserted the homing bees. Soaring straight up, Shannon's pod left his pursuers confused and off-course. As they fought to control the forward thrust of their own ships, the Patrollers found themselves nearly a mile away from their target. They banked, most of them, a few minutes later, and darted upward after Shannon.

The time Shannon had gained by his abrupt manoeuvre was sufficient. His pod nosed its way into the underbelly of the mother-ship. The trap closed behind it.

Like a perfectly timed watch, the mother-ship fired its rockets an instant after the pod had entered the bay area. In minutes, it was out of the atmosphere and free of Earth's gravitational pull.

Shannon ate that night, not alone in his cabin as was his usual custom, but in the crew's mess. His words were curt, but they carried his message of gratitude and congratulations. The crew, to a man, merely accepted what they knew was their due.

Later, he asked Starson how successful they had been.

'We got one hundred and seventy-two this time,' Starson replied. 'Rawley is transplanting them now.'

Shannon nodded, pleased. Now he had the full quota his contract called for, with a comfortable few to spare. He ordered the ship's course set for the planet Ra and then went down to the cargo hold. He patted the sweating Lee Rawley on the back, and together the two men stared in silence at their treasure. The mice were encapsulated in tiny glass cubicles, tier after tier of them. And, encapsulated now within the wombs of the mice, were the stolen human eggs. They were safe and secure for the journey to Ra, where Bernie Lennett awaited their delivery. Upon arrival on Ra, the human eggs would be removed from the mice and transplanted into artificial wombs, which would carry the embryos to term. Long before that time, Shannon would have been paid and would have left.

'Thanks, Rawley,' Shannon said. 'It was a helluva good haul.'

'One of the girls died,' Rawley said. 'Shock.'

'But you got the egg?'

'I did.'

Shannon smiled. 'I've got a surprise for you.'

'Nothing surprises me, Shannon.'

'We're stopping at Seventh Heaven for a while on the way to Ra. Call it a bonus for the crew.'

Rawley remained silent.

Shannon left him and went to his cabin, where he lay down, his hands behind his head, his mind adrift in dreams of money and all that money could buy. What had Rawley said? That a girl had died? But Rawley had got the egg in time. Good man, Rawley.

Sleep came like a virgin to Shannon, wary and shot through with fears.

As the darkness closed around him, he thought about Seventh Heaven and was almost happy.

CHAPTER TWO

Seventh Heaven appeared first on the scanscreen of Shannon's ship as nothing more than a globule of white light that flashed into being, turned pink and then red, to indicate diminishing distance between itself and the ship, and then disappeared altogether as the ship began its docking manoeuvres.

Seventh Heaven, through the viewplates, looked like a cluster of glowing jewels carelessly strewn about in the spacelanes. Shannon, as he stared at it while the ship was on automatic, imagined it as nothing more than what it was. He was not dizzied by its multilevel construction, its glittering radiance, or the enticing sensory waves it beamed out to nearby ships. He knew it simply for what it was. He knew it for a place of anchorage where ships – and just possibly souls – might find both lusty surcease and a temporary haven. He knew it for the bizarre bordello it was.

At Shannon's elbow, a yellow light winked up at him. He acknowledged its message. He pushed, in intricate sequence, a series of buttons. Outside the viewplate, Seventh Heaven rose and tilted, turned and danced to the left and then to the right as the ship descended and entered the docking site. Shannon watched as the site doors slid open to receive the ship. The action — the act of docking — brought a rumble of laughter out of his throat. Perhaps they had designed it that way — symbolic and sensuous. Doubtful. He decided that it was only his overactive glands feeding his brain with the fuel of desire that allowed him to interpret the simple technological act of docking and mooring a spaceship as the sexual thrust and lunge of a man into the symbolically feminine opening of the dock doors.

'Starson!' he bellowed, rising and walking back through the passage to the row of cabins where the crew was quartered. 'We're here. Where the hell are you?'

He finally found Starson, alone as usual, on the lower cargo deck. He was leaning against the thick glass panel that separated him from the tiny cubicles on the opposite side in which the living cargo scratched and gnawed and sucked the minuscule nipples from which a nutrient solution constantly seeped. The cargo — the slightly more than four hundred mice — were the usual white, black, and patchwork mice, plus a few pink ones. They were, Shannon thought, as he watched Starson watching the mice, the ideal animal for his purposes. They were small, and that was their most important qualification. They could be shipped easily anywhere in the galaxy and beyond it with little trouble — hundreds of them, each of their wombs sheltering several fertilised human eggs. Cows wouldn't do. Too big. Even dogs or cats would reduce the important quantitative factor in Shannon's business and thereby measurably reduce his net profit. He had tried transportation in artificial wombs, only to find that their instability factor during spaceflight caused the eggs to atrophy. No, live mice were the obvious answer. They made his business profitable, and that was Shannon's only concern.

What was Starson doing? He barely breathed. Shannon could not see his face. Starson came down here often when he was off duty. Shannon saw nothing fascinating about the mice. They were just . . . mice.

'Starson.'

Starson turned around slowly. 'Shannon, did you say there were over a thousand this time?'

'Eggs? Yes. One thousand and sixteen. Why?'

'One thousand and sixteen,' Starson repeated. His brown eyes flickered beneath their heavily lashed lids. His hands, his fingers, moved slightly, as if they were counting, in the way of unsure children in the early years of school. He was slender, but his slenderness was deceptive. It did not spell weakness. His body was strong and muscular, his bones not large but decidedly serviceable. His grip was firm, and his fists had met more than one opponent's face and body with unpleasant results for those opponents. 'One thousand and sixteen. So many.'

'We've carried more.'

'I know.'

'Over two thousand last time out to Aldebaran. Tell me something. Why do you come down here? Why do you watch the mice?'

Starson grinned and ran his hand through the forest of his black hair. The several rings on his fingers flashed in its tangle, and the tan of his hand was mahogany in an ebony nest. He shrugged. 'I like living things. They fascinate me. I mean . . . well, I don't know, really.'

Shannon shrugged. 'You're at liberty,' he said. 'We've docked.'

'Seventh Heaven?'

'All seven heavens.'

'To each his own, Shannon?'

Gruffly, angrily, Shannon said, 'Secure the ship before you set one wayward foot off her. Forcefield her.' He stood his ground, aware that he was glaring at Starson, aware that the hard edge of his anger was somewhat blunted by another, gentler feeling that lurked somewhere in the shadowy chambers of his mind and which he would not or could not name.

Starson stepped around Shannon and made his way down the passage, his hand trailing along the clear and shining glass behind which the mice nuzzled and scurried. He went through the door and around the corner.

Coincident with his disappearance, Lee Rawley arrived from the opposite direction and greeted Shannon with a nod. 'How long are we going to be here, Shannon?' he asked, as he busied himself adjusting the dials on the feeding apparatus that sustained the mice.

Shannon didn't reply at first. Starson — their encounter — had left him feeling uneasy. He felt familiar and dark demons stirring within him somewhere. *Damn Starson!*

'Daydreaming—' Rawley stood facing Shannon, an eyebrow lifted slightly, the corners of his mouth turned up in what was not quite a smile.

'Nightmaring,' Shannon replied. 'What did you say?'

'I asked how long we would be staying here. What's our schedule?'

'Twelve hours. It should be enough. It'll have to be. How's the cargo?'

'Splendid, although we did lose a few mice in the last day or two.'

'Present egg count?'

'One thousand and six. We've lost four mice — ten eggs in all.'

'Our contract calls for the delivery of one thousand. Don't lose any more.' Shannon strode down the passage and around the corner.

In his cabin, he stripped off his clothes and stepped into the shower. The steam that swirled up in the enclosure was pleasantly warm and languid. Counterbalancing it was the invigorating cold water he turned on after he had washed himself thoroughly. He dried himself with blasts of hot air and stepped out of the shower and into his far-from-princely cabin.

There was little if anything princely about the ship or its accommodations.

It was an old ship which he had bought years ago after his first one had been damaged beyond repair. A meteor had exploded in its path and punctured the hull like blasts of birdshot. This present ship had been retired from service as a long-run freighter and had been up for auction at the Federal Preserve on Marstation when Shannon arrived in port. Its purchase had taken nearly every Token he had had at the time. It wasn't a bad bargain, really. He needed a cargo carrier for his purposes. He later borrowed enough Tokens — a few here, a few there — to make the necessary adjustments in the cargo hold that he required, and he was back in business. His last trip out when the meteor had struck had been a financial disaster. He had lost his cargo — all of it — thereby voiding his contract. Every mouse on board had perished. The meteor fragments had penetrated the air filtration system, and the mice had all been asphyxiated. They couldn't protect themselves by switching on auxiliary filtration as Shannon and the crew had done in their quarters after the collision. Shannon blamed himself for what had happened. He had not got to the mice in time. He had shanghaied his astrogator that trip, and the man, Shannon still suspected, had deliberately plotted their course to coincide with the track of the meteor racing towards them. The astrogator had been about to marry before Shannon subjected him to Mythmadness and had him carted aboard. For days afterwards, the man had raved and stormed about the ship, threatening to foul the navigation system with sugar crystals. Shannon fought him finally, fist to fist, and afterwards the man performed his duties in a silence that was a cool pool of hatred.

Shannon, with a grim smile, put aside his memories. He chose a silk shirt and velvet trousers, both yellow. As he slid his long legs into the trousers and then belted them about him, he faced himself in the mirror. He was definitely not handsome, he realised, principally due to the scar on his face, which had been one legacy of that battle to end all battles in which he had engaged in the hold of his first ship when he had been an honest man — an executive officer in the Space-lane Five Fleet, in fact. There had been an attack by freelane pirates. Lasers and long knives had been the weapons they used. A knife had midwifed the scar, opening his face like a piece of bloody, butchered beef. The limp that plagued him was also the result of that encounter. A laser beam had broken both flesh and bone in his left leg during the mêlée, and no surgeon had ever been able to weld the bones together again in a way that would let him walk normally.

He stared at his reflection in the mirror without pity or any real regret. No, he wasn't handsome. His hair was too thick and too wiry, and it wasn't black or brown, but some-thing rather nondescript in between. His eyes were a pale blue, not unlike the eyes of an albino. At times he speculated on the genetic message they signalled. What had happened back there in the timestack of days and nights, and between whom, that had left him with the legacy of a pair of ghostly, blue-white eyes? He would never know. He bent down and pulled on a pair of boots, thinking of Starson, forgetting him-self.

Starson was twenty-seven years old, only three years younger than Shannon himself. But he was like a twelve-year-old with his clear and unlined skin. The aura of youth was a bright corona about him. Only Starson's eyes betrayed him. They were the eyes of a centenarian. They had seen too much too often, and it showed.

Shannon shoved his hands in his pockets. He glanced at himself in the mirror again, not wishing he were handsome or that he walked as steadily as any other man, but wishing that he ... The thought wouldn't come clear. He couldn't even think the wish. But it was there. A yearning. Someday he would surprise it in the shadows within his brain and know exactly what it was he wished.

There was something in his pocket. A piece of paper. He withdrew it and unfolded it.

'I knew you'd choose the yellow outfit. But I bet you put on your old garrison belt. Take it off. In the second drawer of your clothes cabinet is a scarlet sash. Put it on.'

18

Shannon crumpled the note and threw it in the waste-disposal unit. It had no signature. It needed none. Shannon knew that Starson had written it. The leather garrison belt he had indeed put on suddenly felt too tight. Studying himself in the mirror, he decided that the belt really wasn't right. It was old and scarred and stained. Like myself, he thought. He wore it because it was familiar, and he liked such familiar, friendly things as old clothes and worn tools. He slipped the belt through the loops of his trousers and tossed it on his bunk. He found the sash, neatly laid out as if waiting for him. It was a narrow piece of silk, brightly red. He threaded it through the loops of his trousers and tied it in a knot at his side, letting the ends hang down unevenly. Looking at himself again in the mirror, he decided that Starson had been right. He looked quite dashing. It was the sash that did it. He grinned faintly before going out and up the ladder to the airlock, on his way to one or more of the seven heavens that waited just outside the walls of his tired old hell of a ship.

CHAPTER THREE

Mirrors.

Quaint instruments.

Scented pools with bright blossoms floating on their surfaces.

Incense and thongs and costumes.

Seventh Heaven was Wonderland, and Alice was everywhere. On one level, she wore high, high heels and carried a riding crop. Another Alice on another level sat astride a throne, and on her head, instead of a crown, was a filmy mourning veil. Countless Alices, seven levels, a boutique of bizarre entertainment, a haven where the dark calls of flesh to flesh — whatever their nature might be — never went unanswered. Seventh Heaven. Refuge and zoo. It was its own world in which penance and pain and love and desire and hate and guilt and fear and trembling blended and fused, lurking one within the other, ever altering, ever deceiving.

As Shannon entered the gilded reception hall, odd music filtered softly through the air to his ears. The wordless song suggested to him the desperate cry of the stricken antelope when the claws of the lion are in its flanks.

He saw the girl coming towards him, and his eyes narrowed appraisingly. Short she was, with up-tilted breasts like ripe apples, and an unmistakable gaudiness in her glance. She looked as if she would be able to endure anything and all things. She reached out, and he let her take his hands in her own.

'Home is the sailor,' she said. 'Home from the seas of space. Was it a long trip?'

Shannon nodded. 'Out from Earth twenty days ago with a good crew, poor provisions, and only our dream of dollars at the end to console us. What's your name?'

The girl, instead of answering, asked a question. 'Are you a pirate?'

Shannon's laughter was without joy. When it had subsided, he thought about the girl's question briefly, and then answered it not in the negative as he had been intending to do, but with an affirmative nod of his head. Well, it was true. He was a pirate of a strange sort, although he had never thought of himself or his occupation quite that way before.

'What do you steal, pirate?'

'I asked your name.'

With no coyness, but with a practised lure in her voice, the girl replied, 'Eve.'

'Let every man be Adam, then,' Shannon said, bowing slightly.

The girl evidently had not expected the compliment, nor to hear it put so gracefully. She seemed surprised that this mountain of a man with the broad shoulders and heavy hands hanging at his sides could turn his tongue to work such graceful subtleties. It obviously pleased her. 'What pleasures can we provide for you? Oh, forgive me. I have not been employed here very long, and I am still learning how to . . . Come, Adam. Come with me.'

The girl, her sleek gown swirling about her sandalled feet, took his arm and led him to the console of little lights and buttons that covered a major portion of one wall of the reception hall. 'The screens are numbered, as you can see,' she told Shannon. 'Press the buttons, and you will see what you can expect on each level. The sights you will see typify the level's orientation, but, I should add, you will not be invading anyone's privacy. We are very conscientious about that here. The scenes were filmed by us earlier, using adroit members of our staff. Let me bring you a drink.'

Shannon felt her release his arm, and he almost regretted her going. It had been nice to feel briefly bound by another human being, however tentatively. The thought disturbed him, and he promptly put it out of his mind. He pressed the button labelled 'Level Four'. Although he had visited Seventh Heaven several times before, he knew that the delights accessible on any given level at any given time were likely to have changed since his previous visit. Variety, the owners of this pleasure palace had long ago learned, was more than just the spice of life. It was also the quality that brought customers back a second and a tenth and a hundredth time and put money in many pockets and a thin joy in as many hearts.

The screen labelled 'Level Four' flickered and glowed into life.

There were two women in the huge bed. Their bodies were carnivals of movement around and about the object of their attentions — the naked man lying indolently on his back, his hands folded behind his head. Hair flying and fingers skilfully touching him now here, now there, the women whirled and writhed above him like dervishes.

Shannon pressed the audio button.

A deep male groan erupted into a higher register and emerged as a great wail. They were turning the man over now. Now he was on his stomach, his arms flung out, his buttocks two white hills above the girl sliding beneath him as the other one bent down towards him and . . .

The girl who had greeted Shannon appeared at his side. 'Here's your drink, pirate.'

He did not hear her. She glanced at the screen. Her face showed no emotion as she placed the drink on the circular table beside the console and quietly withdrew.

Shannon darkened the screen of Level Four a few minutes later. As he did so, he noticed the drink the girl had brought. He drank it all in one long gulp and lighted Level One after a moment of obvious hesitation. He had been about to pass it by.

The walls of the room were granite and slate. Embedded in them were iron chains from which manacles hung and above which torches burned in evenly spaced niches. The floor of the room was wet and glistening. Into the empty room came three men, naked except for the hip-high boots and leather vests they wore. In the hands of two of the men were slick whips ending in tightly braided thongs. The whip carriers embraced eagerly, kissed, and then turned to their companion, who seemed to acquiesce to their unheard demand, dropping to his knees as he did so. The two men dragged him to the wall and fastened the manacles about his wrists raised their whips, and brought them singing down upon him.

Shannon brought his fist down hard upon the button, and the screen went dark.

Level Seven.

She was asleep, or seemed to be, on a pile of furs in the middle of a mirrored room. Beside her a fountain tossed a watery mist mixed with tiny flowers into the still air. Her long hair sprayed out over the hides on which she lay. It was the colour of old, old gold and looked as soft as the rushes of a marsh on Earth. Her nose was straight, with small nostrils above her slightly parted lips that were full and had been touched with a delicate pastel lip pomade. Her long eyelashes feathered her pale cheeks.

Shannon felt lust awaken in his loins. The girl wore a gown of white that was more translucent than transparent. Had she been nude, he would not have felt such desire for her, he was certain. But the gown that flowed over her body like a cascade of sea froth hinted at the marvel of her beneath it without revealing her every secret too soon or too completely.

He heard the faint hum that came from something striking something else — perhaps a ball of chamois against thin brass — a gong.

Her eyes were amber, he saw, as she opened them. She stretched, running impossibly long and slender fingers through the fur on which she was lying. In a movement like rippling water, she rose and went behind an Oriental screen. Impatiently, Shannon waited for her to return.

When she did, a man was with her. Before he recognised the man, hidden as he was in total familiarity, he recognised the yellow velvet trousers belted with a scarlet sash that the man was wearing. *Himself!*

How ... ?

The girl who had greeted him earlier when he arrived appeared beside him to answer his unspoken question. 'You were photographed when you arrived. The camera is linked to our computer, where your probable actions were selected from among numerous possibilities, and the holographic display was then programmed for your entertainment. We decided to show you what awaits you with Reba Charlo.'

'Reba Charlo. How much does she cost?'

The girl named a figure that was at least four times as much as Shannon had expected but which he was more than willing to pay. Reba Charlo, he thought, would be worth every Token.

On the screen, he watched himself remove the tiny golden clasps that fastened Reba's gown at her shoulders. The gown slipped free and slid down, to hang in folds about her waist. Shannon stared at himself staring at Reba. The screen Shannon unbound the buckles resting on her hips, and the gown puddled to the floor. She stepped out of it, brushed her hair

23

back from her shoulders with a gesture that was vibrant and faintly bestial. She moved towards him. He took her in his arms, took all the majestic beauty of Reba Charlo, and, watching himself, felt himself enter a roaring volcano that seared his mind and inflamed his senses.

'I want Level Seven,' he told the girl firmly.

'You want Reba Charlo,' the girl said. 'Reba is Level Seven. She has taken booty from many pirates before you. She is our choicest offering at the present time to those of our clients who prefer women — one at a time.'

Shannon handed the girl his cashcard. She quickly verified his balance in the bank on Marstation via her computer credit terminal, unaware that the name he had given her was false. He used the name Ackerman to maintain the Marstation account.

'The lift is to your left,' the girl said. 'Through that door, and then to the left. Enjoy yourself, pirate.'

Shannon followed the girl's directions and found himself in front of the pneumatic lift, which carried him soundlessly, a moment later, upwards to Level Seven and Reba Charlo.

As he entered the apartment designated as Level Seven, he felt like a pirate come to plunder, and the treasure that was the object of his search reclined across the room from him on a low couch covered with purple brocade. She was more beautiful in person than she had appeared on the screen in the reception area. She was wearing a one-piece suit of some veloured fabric that clung to her body.

'Your name is Shannon,' she said. Her voice was faintly husky but totally feminine. 'First name or last?'

'John Shannon.' Her greeting unnerved him. Hadn't he given the girl in the reception room the false name of Ackerman? He had. Then how did Reba Charlo know his name was Shannon?

'I know your name is Shannon,' she told him, 'and I know other things about you as well. I know they call you the Mythmaster and that you are the prize fly that the spider Oxon Kaedler covets.'

Shannon stood rigidly in front of her, unsure of himself

24

suddenly and hating his uncertainty when he should be confident and commanding.

'Starson,' Reba said and smiled. 'He is here too.'

Shannon looked around the room.

'Oh, no! Not *here*.'

She got up and went to the decanter on the table near her couch. She poured a glistening green liqueur into two small glasses and held one out to Shannon, who stepped forward and took it from her. 'Starson,' she said, 'is here in Seventh Heaven, as are the other members of your crew. I know Starson well and have known him for a long time. As you might expect, if you know him at all, he is on Level One. I am told they have imported a number of very handsome and very agreeable young men from Earth to staff that level. Starson is with them.'

'I'm not surprised.'

'Nor should you be. Not everyone is born with blue eyes. Not everyone likes caviar. Not everyone dreams the same dreams. He is in love with you, you know.'

'I know.'

Shannon sipped the liqueur. A tang brought his tongue to vivid life. He drained the glass. 'I hired him as my astrogator. I don't hate him.'

'But you don't love him, either.'

'No, I don't.' Shannon hesitated and then said, 'I'm here. I've chosen you.'

Reba's eyes grew wide with pretended ingenuousness. 'Why, Shannon? Why me and not Starson?'

'I don't want to talk about Starson. His appetites are not mine and never have been.'

'But you are so tolerant of him and his appetites. So very kind.'

She was mocking him. He knew it. He had come to make love to her. He was beginning to need to hate her.

'You are furious with me, John Shannon. Come here. Look at yourself in the mirrors. See how your eyes flash! And look there. Your hands are fists. I shall tease you no more. How very exciting you look in yellow. The sash Starson recommended — very nice. Yellow is your colour. But you would look equally attractive in green or violet. You would look good — remember, I am experienced in these matters — in only the tight, taut skin that hides you from the world. In only that.'

Shannon felt the knot of fury that had been growing within him begin to loosen. He put down his empty glass and took off his shirt. He sat down and pulled off his boots.

Reba poured herself another drink. As he stood up and began to unzip his trousers, she laughed.

Shannon stared at her, his fingers waylaid in their attempted action.

'Shannon, you are not like Starson. Nor, I imagine, are you like the rutting spacers in their clumsy search for sex. For your own sake as well as mine, let me recommend that you not ungird yourself for battle so soon or so matter-of-factly. Come and touch the lobes of my ears first. Place your hard hands upon my breasts. I shall turn on some music. I shall pour more liqueur for us. We will move about each other slowly until our orbits join with a sweet inevitability. Do not seek to plough so fertile a field as myself before our sun has had a chance to rise.'

Sheepishly, Shannon slipped his boots back on. This was a mistake, he decided. Reba Charlo was a mistake. There were other levels where the women would not talk so much, where they would not make a man know his own clumsy failures. He made up his mind. If this was not to be the idyll he had imagined, it would be, nevertheless, a few hours to remember. And if the memory must be base, he was not to blame. Reba was.

'Come here,' he said in a low tone.

Without hesitation, Reba came to stand in front of him. She was nearly as tall as he was, and seemed as invulnerable. It showed, her invulnerability, in the cold depths of her eyes. The coldness there contradicted without entirely cancelling the warmth her body projected. Shannon wondered what kind of thoughts were going on in her mind. He suspected that they were calculating and perhaps cruel. But he did not really care.

'I have paid,' he reminded her, 'although your price is planet-high. When I pay for merchandise, I expect prompt delivery and complete satisfaction. Begin.' He felt triumph spread through him as he felt her fingers touch his bare chest as she leaned forward and kissed his throat.

'There are things I think about in the long times between space stations,' he said. 'Wild and barbaric things.'

'I can be both wild and barbaric.'

'With only the cold stars for companions, a man begins to imagine things. Warm things. Soft things. Women. Women waiting for a man to come and be fulfilled with them. Women offered for sale on auction blocks while the slave dealer winks at potential buyers. I have bought you.'

There was no more music, no more liqueur. Shannon deliberately stripped their meeting of any possible gentility. Something had gone very wrong from the moment he had entered Reba's apartment. He told himself that it did not matter. They were here, he and his crew, for twelve hours. He had paid for Reba Charlo. He would be back here in the months and even years to come, and there would be other Rebas with different names. She would probably be gone to some dark place where wrinkles did not show and faded flesh was no liability. He too would be old in those years yet to be. But the girls who would take Reba's place would all be young and pliant, and if he could still pay their price, he would still receive quality performances from any or all of them, despite his age. The thought brought him comfort.

He held himself in abeyance while he let his body respond to Reba's ministrations as he stood naked some minutes later in the middle of the room. In the mirrored walls and floor and ceiling, a thousand other Shannons were serviced in intricate ways by a thousand other Rebas, while outside Seventh Heaven, stars were born and stars died, all unnoticed.

He led her at last to the bed in the adjoining room. He came down hard upon her and expertly impaled her. He felt her fighting him, not with her body, which responded readily

27

to his own above hers, but with her spirit. Love was not the result of their union. They were wild animals engaged in a deadly battle to the death.

And afterwards, Reba remained totally untouched. Shannon knew that he had failed in an unknown but important way. Somewhere inside herself, she had hidden from him. The woman he had held in his arms possessed no identity and was therefore unpossessable.

As he was about to leave, Reba, smiling, kissed him one last time.

'You are scarred,' she whispered, running her fingers down the welt that reached from his cheek to his chin.

He understood what she was really saying. He was indeed scarred. She had defeated him by refusing to give anything at all of herself, although she had faultlessly obeyed his every order.

'Say it,' he said. 'Only you and I will hear the words. Say it You'll feel better for it.'

She said nothing for a long moment, looking into his eyes, appraising him. Then she spoke the three evenly spaced words that had lain between them throughout the long hours like sharp daggers. 'I hate you.'

'I know. Good-bye.'

He was in the lift when the red light flashed to declare that Seventh Heaven was being invaded by members of the Space Patrol. He willed the lift downwards. He knew the Patrollers were not looking for a vice arrest. Seventh Heaven paid them too well and often for that. He thought he knew what they were looking for.

Him.

And his mice.

CHAPTER FOUR

Shannon came warily through the doors of the lift as they whispered open in front of him. He saw that the corridor leading to the reception area was guarded by several members of the Space Patrol. He adjusted his trousers ostentatiously, brushed back his hair, and sauntered down the corridor.

The reception area was crowded. He noticed Lee Rawley being questioned by a Patroller on one side of the large room. Others of his crew were also present — Maxevitch, Devlin, one or two more, some looking sheepish, some looking sly. Maxevitch, when he spotted Shannon, gave a barely perceptible nod. The motion declared that things could be better.

Shannon headed for the exit. A uniformed Patroller snarled a single curt command, backed up by a very visible and very dangerous laserlight that he held firmly in his right hand. Shannon halted, turned, smiled.

The Patroller did not return the smile. He beckoned to Shannon, who came limping forward, the scar on his face whiter than usual.

'Name?' asked the Patroller.

'Ackerman,' Shannon lied pleasantly. 'I was delayed up above. Seventh Level.' He jerked a thumb at the ceiling and winked at the ramrodded man whose laserlight remained unholstered in his hand. 'Listen, I'm in a helluva hurry. I don't want to miss the shuttle back to Marstation.'

'There is no shuttle docked here,' the Patroller commented coolly.

'God damn!' Shannon exclaimed. 'I must have missed it! When's the next one due in?'

Before the Patroller had time to answer, another one entered the room from the direction of the dock site. He saluted

29

the officer who had been interrogating Shannon and said, 'The old freighter moored out there may be the one we're looking for. It's got no fleet designation, and it's force-fielded. It may belong to the Mythmaster.'

'No designation,' mused the Patroller. 'Then it's an illegal vessel by definition, according to Code.' He paused, not quite looking at Shannon. 'Disintegrate the ship.'

Shannon sprang at the man and gave a wild yell that included a few words and Starson's name. Starson, who was at that moment being led into the area by another Patroller, found Shannon's yell to be signal enough. He needed no further cue nor encouragement. He whirled around, freed himself from the Patroller's grip on his tunic, and felled the man with a single jarring jolt from his right fist, followed by an ignoble knee to the man's groin. The Patroller cried out and toppled to the floor, clutching himself and groaning. Starson, his face afire and his white teeth flashing in a grin that displayed the emerald set in one front tooth, leaped over the fallen man and ran towards Shannon. He seized the surprised Patroller beside Shannon and pressed adroitly with strategically placed thumbs, and unconsciousness came down upon the Patroller with the speed of a tropical night.

Shannon sent a third Patroller spinning away from him, to fall heavily against the screen console. 'Rawley!' he yelled. 'Maxevitch! Now!'

The room became a zoo in which the animals, uncaged, roared and fled, stampeded and attacked one another. A laser-light flashed in the midst of the tumbling bodies. With an eerie whine, a section of the screen console split apart and melted. Starson howled and brawled his way past one fallen Patroller, bounced off another, and sent a third into temporary oblivion by locking his head and arms among the lower rungs of the airlock ladder.

Shannon, beside him, led the way to the alternate exit. The rest of the crew was not far behind. Shannon turned to look back, to shout encouragement to them. He saw Devlin running towards him. He saw, behind Devlin, a Patroller raise himself groggily on a wavering elbow and aim his laserlight.

'Devlin!' Shannon shouted, dropping to his knees in a defensive crouch. 'Down, man. *Down!*'

The beam flashed out from the laserlight and touched Devlin's back. It passed through him, melting flesh and bone, bursting organs and draining life. Devlin jerked and swayed, and the commingled pain and surprise on his face masked the coming of death only momentarily.

Shannon swore. Dead, his best technician. The Patrollers were entering behind him. He ran back to the ladder and saw booted feet descending. He scurried up the ladder and seized the first foot that had appeared and jerked it, leaping to the floor as he did so. The Patroller came tumbling down, and Shannon grabbed the man's helmeted head and banged it once, twice against the steel floor, until the man no longer moved or moaned.

Starson, still grinning, yelled to Shannon from his precarious perch on the opposite side of the ladder down which more Patrollers were now scurrying. One word he cried: '*Mythmadness!*' He took from his tunic a tiny black globule that glistened in the bright light of the room.

Shannon shouted, 'Now!'

The globule flew forcefully from Starson's hand and shattered on the floor. In a moment, the mist of *Mythmadness* filled the room.

'Rawley!' Shannon bellowed. 'Maxevitch! *Mythmadness!*'

Rawley, who had been dancing lithely out of the path of several pursuing Patrollers, reached in his pocket and thrust his hand against his mouth. Maxevitch did the same. Shannon and Starson swallowed their own antidote capsules, which would make them immune to the effects of the Mythmadness that was about to begin.

It began with the delicacy of spring in the interiors of the Earth. As subtly and as remarkably. A Patroller who had been lunging forward like an enraged bull towards the lock ladder suddenly slowed in his tracks, and a quizzical expression replaced the fury that had, only moments before, twisted his features. He moved slightly to the left, taking a dainty step, an incongruous one, considering his size. He moved then to the right, taking first a short step and then a longer one. He turned. He bent, bowed, straightened, and went on with the intricate steps of the dance he was performing to music that only he could hear.

It was working. Mythmadness had invaded Seventh Heaven, and the results were more curious than anything that took place on any level of the pleasure palace.

In the distance, at the end of the corridor, two of the girls from one of the levels crouched as if over an invisible campfire and crooned a wordless song to each other while making motions in the air that were both mystical and beyond any understanding but their own. They rose and stretched towards the ceiling and then dropped to all fours, shaking their heads and growling harshly. They circled each other, their teeth bared, their eyes measuring each other, opponents now in an unknown battle born in the fumes of the chemical hallucinogen that Starson had released.

A Patroller stood against the wall of the corridor. Over and over he muttered, 'Bird thou never wert . . . bird thou never wert . . .' while water streamed down his cheeks from his emptying eyes, and water also streamed down his thighs, staining and darkening his trousers. He grew rigid, while his mind wobbled, enslaved as it were by the fears and deadly dreams he had never before allowed to escape from the secure cellular dungeon of his brain.

'Shannon?'

Shannon, leaning against the ladder, looked up. Starson, standing on the other side of the ladder several feet above him, had stuck his head through the rungs and was grinning down at Shannon like a disembodied creature of the Mythmadness he had created.

'You okay, Shannon?'

'Okay, yes. You?'

Starson's lips parted, and the emerald glittered in his tooth. 'I'm just fine. What a damned shame that we had to turn Seventh Heaven into hell.'

Shannon swivelled around, looking for Maxevitch, Rawley, and the rest of the crew. Maxevitch was leading a

Patroller like a dog on a leash which he had made from a tasselled drapery cord. The Patroller was hopping along, salivating and barking. Rawley staggered towards Shannon, holding his arm, out of breath. Blood leaked through his fingers from the wound in his arm. As he came abreast of Shannon, he said, 'They didn't get their pound of flesh. But they did get an ounce or two of mine.'

Shannon looked at Rawley's wound. 'It's not serious. Up you go.'

Rawley climbed the ladder and disappeared through the lock.

'Maxevitch!' Shannon shouted. 'Out!'

Maxevitch promptly dropped the tasselled drapery cord that served as a leash and patted the Patroller's head one last time. He bounded towards the ladder and then up it, past Shannon and Starson, laughing happily.

When the rest of the crew, with the exception of the dead Devlin, had left Seventh Heaven, Shannon began to climb the ladder after them, with Starson following.

They both halted in their ascent at the sound of someone calling Shannon's name.

Shannon looked around and saw Reba framed in the light at the end of the corridor. Her features were blurred with the light behind her, her body shadowy, but he could tell she wore no gown, no slippers, and her hair was undone, as it had been when he had first met her on Level Seven.

'Come on, Shannon,' Starson said. 'Leave her alone until the Mythmadness passes.'

Shannon paid no attention. He descended the ladder, shoving Starson aside. He moved towards Reba, who still stood motionless at the end of the corridor. What was she saying? What was she whispering? His name.

'Shannon,' she sighed. And again, 'Shannon.'

'Shannon!' Starson yelled after him. 'Before the Mythmadness ends, let's . . .'

But Shannon continued walking down the corridor. The closer he came to Reba, the more her loveliness fired his mind and body. She was obviously Mythmad.

'He is called Shannon,' she was saying to no one, her eyes focused on an inner landscape. 'He is Master of Myth.'

Shannon touched the nipples of her breasts. 'I am Shannon,' he said, 'the Master of Myth. Who are you?'

'Who can tell me?'

'The whore of Babylon,' Shannon said. 'Citizen of Sodom. Girl of Gomorrah.'

'It is so.'

'A lamb to the slaughter.'

'Who brings the knives to rend me? Who is it that brutalises me?'

'My name is Shannon.'

'Do you come from my country? I seem to remember you with your legs like pillars and your heart a locked citadel. Shannon you call yourself, but I remember a bitter fruit into which I bit, and the juices still stain my soul.'

Shannon's hands fondled her face as she gazed at him. He wondered if she were really seeing him. Did she remember him? He decided that she probably did not. She could not remember someone she had never really met and certainly never really known. Her beauty was overwhelming. He wanted her. Here. Now. Again. She was passive as he embraced her. Her fires were banked. In her Mythmadness her passion was a wilted flower out of season.

'He wanted me to hate him,' she said. 'So I said I did. Such a sad thing. He suffers so. I sense it.'

Shannon released her, thrust her from him so suddenly that she faltered, lost her balance, and almost fell.

'Tell him,' she whispered, when she had recovered her balance. 'Tell him, should you meet this Shannon, that I . . .' She stopped speaking and stared at Shannon as if she finally saw him. A cloud disappeared from the suns of her eyes. 'I hate you,' she said flatly, tonelessly.

Shannon heard the sound of faraway trumpets, but he refused to answer their imaginary summons. The game had begun on Level Seven, and he did not know where it would end or who would win it. Words were a part of their game.

Her words and his. They both knew it. It was now his move. 'I hate you,' he said.

'You have to,' she said.

'You bastard, Shannon!' It was Starson, standing beside them. He looked as if he were about to weep — or kill. 'Don't use her, Shannon. She is nothing to you. No one is anything to you, because you won't — or can't — let them be. Leave her alone.' He went quickly to a couch at the entrance to the reception area and returned carrying its silken cover. He placed it around Reba's shoulders and draped it about her body. He took her hands and placed them in such a way that they managed to hold the robe around her body, shielding it from Shannon's gaze.

Shannon shrugged.

'We have a run to make to Ra,' Starson said, positioning himself between Shannon and Reba. 'We have a contract with the colonists there. Our cargo is committed to them.'

Shannon turned abruptly and went towards the ladder.

Starson, staring at Reba, said, 'We will come again. One always returns to the scene of one's crime. Mine is here. Yours is here. And now, so is Shannon's. We three are linked together now. Good-bye.' He bent and kissed her, and her hand rose up slowly and touched his face as if it were a map on which she might locate the path from which she had strayed in search of . . . what?

'Good-bye,' she whispered. 'I too must go now. I have appointments to keep.' She turned languidly and walked past the still-barking Patroller that Maxevitch had trained, past the two girls who now lay locked in each other's arms in a deep and insensate slumber, past the Patroller who stood as if nailed to the wall, arms outstretched, still murmuring, 'Bird thou never wert . . .' and disappeared around the corner.

Starson, when she had gone, hurried to the ladder and went up into the lock. When he boarded the ship, he found Shannon in his cabin staring through the viewplate at Seventh Heaven.

As Starson entered, Shannon said, 'Reba seemed to know you.'

'We met years ago on one of the offworlds where we were both born. We were both very young then. Later, we married.'

'Married!' Shannon exclaimed, whirling around to face Starson. 'You? To a woman? To that magnificent woman?'

A wry smiled appeared on Starson's face. 'Yes. We were in love and in need of each other. But our needs grew in different directions. Each of us is alone now.'

Shannon turned back to the viewplate.

'Did you enjoy her, Shannon?'

'Check the condition of the cargo. Prepare for unmooring before the Mythmadness out there dissipates.'

'If you didn't, perhaps I could — '

Shannon didn't let him finish. 'You are both swine! You and your Reba!'

'To alter the image slightly, Shannon, may I point out that birds of a feather . . .'

Shannon struck him with a fisted hand. But Starson, as his upper lip broke and blood trickled from it, didn't strike back. Shannon tried desperately to hate him for that and failed.

CHAPTER FIVE

Starson stood for a long moment in front of Shannon, pressing a handkerchief to his bloodied lip, and then he turned and left the cabin.

Rawley entered backwards, gazing after Starson, who was striding down the corridor. He turned around and saw Shannon and said, 'I didn't know Starson had been wounded in our little fracas.'

'It's nothing serious,' Shannon said, sitting down in the viewing cradle, which creaked beneath his weight.

Rawley said, 'He's one of our best crewmen. Loyal. Works hard without concern for shift time. Efficient, too.'

'Did the meditech patch you up?'

Rawley nodded, touching the bandage on his bare arm, from which his uniform had been shorn away. 'Men like Starson are an unusual breed. I mean,' he continued quickly, anticipating misinterpretation on Shannon's part, 'I mean that they aren't looking for the easy job or the lazy pace. They're hard workers is what I mean.'

'Yes, he's unusual,' Shannon agreed. 'So are volcanic eruptions. The unusual in and of itself is not necessarily desirable.'

Orchids in Iceland,' Rawley countered.

'Tarantulas on the snow,' Shannon responded. 'Look. The luminosity of Seventh Heaven is altering.'

Rawley leaned over and stared through the viewplate at the glittering mass that was the bordello they had just left. It was spinning away from them as if they had thrown it aside in ennui or perhaps disgust. 'The Mythmadness must still be operative,' he commented. 'Someone must be meddling with the solar generator. That would account for those bursts of light.'

'Did you see her, Rawley?'

'I saw her.'

'Her name is Reba Charlo.'

'She looks like a figure from a Gauguin. She looks as if she were made of light.'

Shannon thought about that. It was a good description of Reba, he decided. He recalled the radiance of her hair that was the dull gold of an approaching sunset. Her skin — so pale, almost translucent. The pomade she used pinked her lips without turning them garish. And the scent that emanated from her was more powerful than myrrh and yet as subtle as the fresh smell of an orchard on Earth. Innocence and sultriness haloed her, as did her pefume.

Within Shannon, within the caldron that was the man, dark juices began to flow and bubble as he thought about Reba. Her obvious amorality was matched only by her apparent invulnerability. Shannon quickly forgot Starson and Rawley. He imagined himself a centaur pawing the ground in some mystical garden. A voluptuous maiden dashed past him through the sun-splintered glade. He caught her, and she succumbed to his urgent and evident need beneath a sky that was abruptly filled with exploding suns of many colours that warmed the sweet and Eden-like air.

He gradually became aware once again of Seventh Heaven through the viewplate, a pointillistic dot now in the emptiness of the spacelane, and he watched it until it winked out, a victim of distance.

He looked up. Rawley was gone. Reba was gone. Starson? Somewhere.

He got up from the creaking cradle and made his way to the command cabin of the ship. As he entered, a junior crewman greeted him with a sloppy salute.

He went to the instrument panel and glanced down at the data concerning cargo condition registered there. 'Who established this temperature and nutrient data?' he asked the crewman.

'Maxevitch, sir.'

'Get him up here.'

The crewman spoke Maxevitch's name into the intercom system, and within minutes Maxevitch appeared in the command cabin.

Shannon pointed to the instrument panel. 'Your data?'

'Yes,' Maxevitch answered readily.

Shannon beckoned to him, and he came to stand beside the panel. 'You miscalculated,' Shannon told him. 'The cargo temperature is two degrees lower than it should be. And the nutrient flow is unstable.'

Maxevitch leaned forward and examined the data. Turning then to Shannon, he said, 'But the temperature is within the safety range, and the solution flow is quantitatively correct, although a bit irregular, I admit.'

'Four mice died in the last few days. We lost ten eggs. Without correct handling of the cargo, more could die and our contract be invalidated. There is a penalty for sloppiness

38

aboard this ship. Sloppiness in some areas could lead to capture by the Patrol and probably solitary confinement in one of their orbiting satellite cells for months or even years. And, in your case, Maxevitch, your sloppiness could mean dead mice, which means dead eggs, which means financial loss. You'll be deprived of your ration of Mythmakers for one week. Starting immediately.'

'But, sir . . . Shannon . . . I . . .'

'You were right the first time.'

Maxevitch dropped his gaze. 'Sir, the Mythmakers are a necessity to anyone addicted, as you know. Deprivation can mean serious sensory aberrations.'

'Such aberrations, as *you* know, are . . .'

'Painful.'

'Such aberrations, as you know, are temporary, although admittedly rather unpleasant. The very point, Maxevitch.' Shannon barked a command into the intercom, instructing the dispensary to note Maxevitch's new status when dispensation of Mythmakers to the addicted members of the crew next took place. Then he nodded curtly, and Maxevitch turned and hurled himself in tight fury from the cabin.

A few minutes later, Shannon went to his own cabin and switched on the telepanel. He examined the interior of his ship. The crew's mess was nearly empty except for the cook and his two miniature civet cats, which were perched together in the air vent. He made a mental note to order the air-vent grid replaced at once. Those damned civet cats! The cook had been warned that no life forms other than human were allowed aboard the ship, with the notable exception of the cargo of mice. But he had evidently succeeded in smuggling the creatures aboard. Shannon decided to say nothing about them for the moment. Should the cook get out of line, as was all too common with cooks aboard ships suffering the dubious status of his own, he would confiscate and threaten to destroy the cats. Everyone had his weakness, Shannon had long ago learned. And long ago he had learned how to turn human weaknesses to his own ultimate advantage.

He redialled the telepanel, and the pod dock came into

39

view. He witnessed, unexpectedly the weakness of Maxe-vitch. The man was stalking the docking area, back and forth, back and forth. His lips were moving, but Shannon did not need to turn up the audiation system to know that what sputtered from the man's mouth were curses. He watched as Maxevitch stopped, rummaged through his pockets, and brought out a container of capsules. Mythmakers. Shannon wondered how many in all Maxevitch might have hoarded. He would make it a point to surprise him in a day or two. At that time, supposedly undergoing withdrawl symptoms, Shannon now knew that he would find Maxevitch blissful and serene in his bunk under the influence of his contraband Mythmakers, which were a milder version of the formula that created Mythmadness. They induced pleasant and usually erotic hallucinations and were physically as well as psychologically addictive. Shannon made up his mind. After the discovery, he would order Maxevitch's forced period of abstinence extended to two weeks.

He redialled the telepanel several times. Everything seemed normal in all the other parts of the ship. Still, he felt dis-satisfied. But hadn't he seen all he needed to see? No, he had not. Rapidly dialling again, Shannon surveyed the crew's shabby cabins. He knew this was forbidden on legal flights. Space was a place where the relatively confined quarters and the long unwinding of time with the same people for too long on most trips demanded that a man be allowed to withdraw to a sanctuary that was not necessarily clean and certainly not holy — the latter a ridiculous idea in crew cabins — but was at least his own and private. Nevertheless, Shannon had installed receptors in all the cabins, disguising them as mirrors.

Where was Starson?

He was not in his cabin. Nor was he in any of the other crewmen's cabins. Shannon switched off the telepanel in an-noyance. He started to leave and then halted. He'd find Star-on in the cargo hold!

He turned on the telepanel again and dialled 'Hold'. At first, he saw only the glass behind which the mice nurtured the secrets that even they did not know. He dialled 'Hold, Interior'.

He spotted Starson crouching beside the exit door. On his knee perched a fat mouse. Peeping from the top pocket of his tunic was another one, its nose quivering, its whiskers flicking. Starson touched the mouse on his knee with one index finger on which a ruby gleamed redly. The mouse seemed to respond to his caress. He enveloped it in his hand, raised it up to his face, and stared into its eyes.

Shannon turned on the audiation system and listened to Starson's sibilant voice.

'*Sing a song of Shannon, sing it till I die. Shannon's sick of singing. And so am I.*'

The mouse in his hand blinked its tiny wet eyes. Starson removed the other mouse from his tunic pocket and stood up. He gently replaced both animals in their cubicles and seemed about to turn away when something attracted his attention. It was his own image in the glass of the tiered cages. He leaned closer to it, his lips almost touching the glass, his breath frosting it. He withdrew from it, raised a finger to his broken lower lip which still bled, and then brought it away from his face. He stared at it. Then, with no smile but an expression of utter loss and hopelessness ruining his handsome features, he touched the glass with his bloodied finger and made a wavering design. Beside it, he made a second similar one.

Shannon studied Starson's small, secret message. Two snaked lines. Meaningless smears, he thought at first. But no. They were letters.

S. S.

Shannon watched as Starson backed away from the glass and moved like a man asleep towards the door.

When he had disappeared, his message remained. Shannon knew what the letters meant. S for Starson. S for Shannon. Side by side but forever apart. No wonder Starson's face had been a dry desert, parched and barren, with the sad knowledge that Shannon would never let him approach the oasis of himself.

S–M–C   41

Shannon stared at the two bloody letters on the glass for another moment and then turned off the telepanel. He sat down on his bunk and propped his feet against the safety mesh surrounding it.

I am the commander of this ship, he thought. I am John Shannon. I am a pirate who steals life and sells it to the highest bidder and asks no questions. I was executive officer of the Spacelane Five Fleet years ago. I will be lifeless one day, perhaps quietly cindered in a crematorium on Earth or on one of the offworlds. I am the Mythmaster, dispenser of dreams and illusions unrequested and just possibly unrequired.

He tensed the muscles in his arms and stretched. He arched his spine. There was no doubt about it. He was real. The safety mesh was real. The ship and this cabin within it were real. Everything in the room had a name, including himself. Door. Wall. Shannon. Bunk.

All pieces of a space/time puzzle. He thought of that other Shannon whom he had mislaid somewhere as he made his not entirely merry way from world to world. That Shannon had been a spit-and-polish mechanism that knew the book and went by it. He had been complimented on his efficiency, promoted rapidly, admired for his tireless energy and quick, correct decisions. The image brought a smile to his lips. Very different were those days from these! Now he sailed a ship that would pass no inspection like those that he himself had once conducted in his executive-officer days. His crewmen seldom saluted him now, and when they did, their gestures were likely to slop over into what could only be called a casual wave or a movement not unlike the flicking away of an unseen insect. There were times when he tried to impose a discipline upon his crewmen which he himself had long ago rejected. No, that was not quite accurate. The discipline characteristic of the Space Patrollers and other legitimate organisations that sailed the lanes was something that, once absorbed into a man's blood, never really left it. That sense of discipline was an antibody against the disease of slovenliness that, in the lanes or on leave anywhere, could lead to death or any number of other disasters. He had not abandoned it, nor

it him. No matter that his ship was dirty and his crew un-
uniformed. When he spoke, they listened. When he commanded, they obeyed. The discipline that he imposed upon
himself crept out to touch his crew, and it gave them,
whether they realised it or not, a sense of safety and an ease
which came of being aware of limits beyond which they
could not go.

He was a fisherman, and money was the gaudy lure that
had netted him his crewmen. Rawley, for example, could
have been a respected member of any university staff, but he
had chosen instead to loose his feet and unfetter his mind,
throw conventional value systems to the winds of all the
worlds, and sail with Shannon. Devlin, now dead, had been
the classical misfit. Unable to hold a job, unable to stay put in
any one place for more than a few months at a time, he had
signed on with Shannon and soon found himself no stranger
to the stars. Maxevitch was a man of many weaknesses, and
he had found in Shannon the one man who would draw lines
which he dare not cross. Shannon's gift to Maxevitch had
been barriers which Maxevitch only dimly sensed he needed,
or else he would find himself established in a hell more hor-
rible than any manufactured by the pellets of Mythmadness.

It was true of all of them. Shannon had walked into their
lives in strange places and at odd moments, and they had
been caught. Trapped? It didn't matter. The hunter, Shannon
suspected, was as much trapped by his prey as was his prey
trapped by him. Accommodation and compromise — these
were the names by which Shannon knew life. Life, for him,
was a market in which countless bargains were constantly
being made. There was only one trick to it all, one he had
learned early in his life, and well. You never got something
for nothing. You had to decide what you wanted and be willing to pay the price for it. You had to convince the man or
woman with whom you bargained that you were not clever,
that you were not shrewd, and that you were not nearly as
sly as you very well knew yourself to be.

Shannon knew himself for a buccaneer and an en-
trepreneur par excellence in the bright bazaar of space. He

was also the master of worlds that never were nor ever would be except within the curious electrical circuitry of human brains — he was the Mythmaster. An interest in control and cash had enabled him to buy the formula for the pellets that created the Mythmadness from a crazed chemist he had met a year ago. The old man had talked much and often of his discovery, but his stubbled face and stained clothes had discouraged belief in his hearers. He had earlier, he said, been expelled from several corporations because of his penchant for a slow and devious suicide which took the obtuse forms of a love for alcohol and a consuming lust for females under the age of fifteen.

But he had perfected his formula and its antidote amid regular bouts with the bottle and frequent orgies which were expensive and lasted only as long as did his little money.

And then he met Shannon in the bar of a spaceport hostel. He said he was not a beggar but had something valuable to sell. So Shannon had bought a bottle for him, knowing that profitable songs could be sung by the most unlikely-looking birds. He listened, not minding the man's sour fragrance or his petulant complaints concerning mistreatment by a world he only wanted to re-make in a glorious and glowing image with the help of his formula. When the man finished speaking, Shannon bought a second bottle and bargained as the man earnestly and repeatedly wheezed out his alcoholic story, coughing and spluttering as he did so.

Shannon hired him to train unskilled labourers to manufacture the pellets and their antidote. Each of the men that had been hired performed but a piece of the overall process, and none of them knew what it was that they were manufacturing.

A week passed during which Shannon procured flesh for the man and generously poured alcohol. At the beginning of the second week, the man, unsated still, died while straddling a blunt-eyed girl who continued placidly eating her orange because she thought the old man's dying shriek meant that he was enjoying himself.

Cardiac arrest. Shannon had calculated correctly once

again — this time concerning the survival potential of the chemist who had been, at the end, something much less than a human being. Shannon had not killed him. Perhaps he had provided weapons. But he had not wielded them. He paid for the cremation of the man's remains and the service that preceded his fiery passage from the scene.

Shannon stretched again and leaned forward to pull off his boots. He undressed and lay down wearily on his bunk. He switched on the tapetext and began listening at the point he had left off the day before.

ANTIGONE: I'll neither urge thee, nor, if now thou'dst help
  My doing, should I thank thee for thine aid.
  Do thou after thy kind: thy choice is made:
  I'll bury him; doing this so let me die.
  So with my loved one loved shall I abide,
  My crime a deed most holy: for the dead
  Longer have I to please than these on earth.
  There I shall dwell for ever: be it thine
  To have scorned what gods have hallowed, if thou wilt.
ISMENE: Nay, nothing do I scorn: but, how to break
  My country's law — I am witless of the way.

The tapetext continued to whisper its words, but Shannon, distracted, put his hands over his eyes.

His distraction bore the name of memory. There had been no one, no loved one, to demand any single sacrifice of him. His mother surrogate had been competent; he had had no quarrel with it. It had lifted the fat basket of flesh that had been his newborn self every half-hour as programmed, and it had fondled him automatically and whispered words he couldn't understand and had plopped its huge plastic breast with its sterilised nipple out and into his mouth, and he had sucked contentedly, feeling himself safe. Then, as the years passed and he was allowed to choose his name and join the other children in the communal nursery, he knew he was not safe because the bloodline that was his would remain forever unknown.

He had chosen his name, John Shannon, from a list they gave him. He chose it by putting a pencil mark at random on one of the pages labelled 'Male'. His name did not matter to him. It would not identify him. Only he would be able to do that in the flow of time in which he would learn to swim with no lifebelt and without hearing the guiding sound of bell buoys.

His life at times seemed as unreal to him as anything released from the pellets out of which the Mythmadness sprang.

He thought of Reba Charlo and wondered if she knew the person who inhabited the lovely castle of her body. And what of Starson and his dark hunger? Did he know who or why he was? Did he know who Shannon was, or did he seek in Shannon the lost shadow of someone else once needed but now gone?

Shannon turned his attention once more to the tapetext.

SENTINEL: Do I afflict thy hearing or thy heart?
CREON: Where I am pained, it skills not to define.

He reached up and switched off the tapetext and lay back in the darkness, feeling the ship around him like a pod in which his life, for the moment, was seeded.

CHAPTER SIX

On the third morning out from Seventh Heaven, Shannon visited the dispensary. 'Who is on sick call?'

The meditech consulted his chart and answered, 'No one.' He added, 'I was expecting some action after our Seventh Heaven stopover a few days ago, but . . . nothing. No urethral complaints. No requests for antibiotics. I did dispense some soporifics.'

'Maxevitch hasn't reported to you?'

The meditech shook his head.

'You logged my order concerning him and the dispensation of Mythmakers?'

Another glance at the chart, and the meditech replied, 'Yes, sir. Right here. He's been off the stuff for over two days now.'

'And he hasn't reported to you — hasn't manifested withdrawal symptoms?'

'No, to the first question, sir. I haven't seen him, so I can't answer the second.'

Shannon left the dispensary and made his way to Maxevitch's cabin. He knocked and received no answer. He tried the door and found it locked, which wasn't abnormal — maybe. 'Maxevitch!' He had checked before visiting the dispensary and learned that Maxevitch had not reported for duty during the last two days. Well, if the man wanted to play the fox, he should have considered every chicken coop. Not reporting for duty was consistent with the problems he would be experiencing under withdrawal from the Mythmakers, but a failure to visit the dispensary made no sense at all under the circumstances.

Shannon used the intercom to summon an assistant engineer. The man came and unlocked the cabin door, after which Shannon dismissed him.

Inside the cabin, Shannon found Maxevitch lying naked on his bunk, a puddle of relaxed flesh on which a thin film of sweat glistened. He shook him. Maxevitch didn't respond. He wasn't sleeping. He was Mythmaking.

Shannon summoned the meditech from the dispensary and gave him instructions. Within minutes the meditch had administered the antidote, and within hours after that, Maxevitch, locked alone in his cabin, could be heard groaning and crying out to anyone and everyone that his eyes were jellied and his ears echo chambers in which he heard all the hideous sins of the world being confessed and would someone please, *please* pluck the needles from his nose — *now*!

47

He grovelled on the floor, which he found covered with a crust of imaginary insects seeking to eat the jelly of his eyes. He heard wicked winds blow, and their insane touch froze his flesh, while his nose, which he imagined was a cluttered nest of needles, scented rotting animal matter and other olfactory agonies.

Shannon, later that day, sat alone in his cabin. He dialled the telepanel and watched Maxevitch. On the audiation system, he heard the sound of a tapetext playing Berlioz in the next cabin. The sound was obviously contributing to Maxevitch's pain. At every crescendo, Maxevitch screamed, and at every swell of the music, he cringed.

Shannon turned off the telepanel and switched on the intercom. 'Attention, all crewmen. Conservation of power is required due to a faulty generator coil. Power is being reduced immediately by four per cent. All tapetexts, unnecessary lights, and appliances are to be turned off at once and will remain off until further notice.'

A few minutes later, the voice of the chief engineer barked through the intercom into Shannon's cabin. 'Sir, there's no faulty generator coil as far as I can tell. Why did you order the power reduction?'

'I was about to call you. Don't worry about the coil. If anyone asks you, tell them you've reduced power by four per cent. But there is no need to actually do so. Understood?'

'Understood.'

Shannon switched on the telepanel again and stared at Maxevitch who was lying huddled on the floor of his cabin. Occasionally he shuddered or clawed weakly at his face. With the tapetext in the next cabin now silent, Maxevitch had only the echoes of his own aberrant organism to contend with until his symptomatology disappeared entirely. Satisfied, Shannon switched off the telepanel.

A week later, Shannon stood beside Bernie Lennett on the planet Ra and watched the unloading of the mice, which were packed safely in thermal containers. The two men were silent, having discovered that the wind on the open tundra tore the words from their lips and whirled them away unheard. In the distance, they heard the ominous growl of the icebergs as they shifted their stiff positions and inched southward.

Bernie slammed his arms, which were bound in thick wads of rags, against his wiry body. 'One thousand?' he screeched, trying to outshout the wind.

Shannon nodded. He held up the fingers of one hand plus one finger on the other.

Bernie puzzled for a moment, and then his flat face, which was normally as dead as the ice that was everywhere, broke into a jubilant grin. 'One thousand and six?' he yelled.

Shannon nodded again.

'How much extra for the six?'

Shannon turned his head, cupped his ear in one hand.

'How much more do I have to pay for the extras?' Bernie screamed.

Shannon held up his hands, his palms turned towards Bernie. He shook his head.

Bernie's jubilation increased. Extra men — or women! And free! There had to be a catch. The Mythmaster didn't give something for nothing. He would wait and make no further reference to the bonus in the hope that Shannon would forget about it.

Shannon withdrew and took shelter in the opening that led to the crumbling space station which served as home, hospital, and gathering place for the people who inhabited Ra. The wind found him, and he shivered. He made up his mind to stay only long enough to collect his fee. There was nothing on Ra to hold him. The cold riveted his bones together and made a bellows of his chest as he struggled to steal a breath from the clutches of the wind and the talons of the ice that were almost visible in the chilling air.

Bernie flapped his arms like an ungainly bird and hopped about on the tundra. As the crewmen carried the thermal packs full of mice past him, he followed Shannon inside. He sat down at once of the long tables that sliced through the long room where meals were eaten communally and where

49

the sun never shone. In place of the sun for which the planet had been named in a futile denial of reality, someone had painted great yellow globes on the black ceiling and on the grimy walls. Looking at them as he sat down beside Bernie, Shannon decided that this was the way religions began — with symbols to protect against known or sensed dangers, with rituals later attached to the symbols so that life would seem more secure.

Bernie leaped to his feet and cried out to the men carrying the packs to take care and to take it easy and to watch out and to mind their steps so that . . .

But no single mouse was damaged. All of them basked comfortably in the controlled heat of their packs.

Bernie hopped, jerked, and skipped, his rags flying from the scarecrow that he seemed to be, down to the far end of the long hall and to the door through which steam was flowing and eddying.

Shannon got up as Bernie beckoned to him, and walked down to the door.

'Look,' Bernie said, pointing with no small amount of pride. 'The vats.'

Shannon peered into the huge room beyond the door, in which he could make out figures moving through swirling clouds of steam. As his eyes became accustomed to the grey murk, he saw that they were hauling huge craggy pieces of ice at the end of rusted iron tongs. They dragged the ice up one of several inclines, and when they reached the top, they pushed them over and down into one of the gigantic metal vats that were suspended by chains from the ceiling and beneath which fires burned in deep pits hollowed out of the ground.

'Up there,' Bernie said, pointing. 'Look.'

Shannon glanced towards the ceiling of the room and saw the catwalk that girdled it. On the walk, sweating women scooped up the thick soupy substance, using long-handled ladles, and poured it into sagging membranes stretched over other, smaller vats.

'The ice contains plankton and algae,' Bernie said. 'We find quite a few edible fossils in it, too. Later, after the transplants are finished, we'll add the mice to it. All in all, it makes a pretty nourishing stew.'

'How do you keep the fires burning?' Shannon asked.

'They're volcanic in origin. They're the main reason we settled here. This is the warmest part of the whole damned planet. We've got a good system worked out, using the natural resources of Ra — the volcanic fires and the ice mines we've established up on the bergs. We're working on a way to pipe the steam farther and farther away from this point so that we can expand our settlement.'

'It's hardly the Garden of Eden.'

'But it's ours, and it's all we've got.'

Shannon smiled. 'The Space Patrol doesn't harass you anymore?'

'Not since the early days. They think we're harmless. Instead of prosecuting us for our mutiny, they seem to have written us off. Do you worry about anthills back on Earth?'

Shannon got the point.

'And this anthill of ours isn't even on Earth, so why should the Patrol bother about us? But they will again in time. Only, by then it will be too late. Thanks in part to you.'

Bernie led the way out of the vat room and back through the long hall to his private compound. He poured a drink and offered it to Shannon.

Shannon sipped it, snorted, and wiped his lips.

'It's made from fermented algae with a bit of volcanic ash added,' Bernie commented. 'It'll put fire in your eyes.'

They toured the remainder of the facilities Bernie and his band had built on Ra. Shannon watched Lee Rawley and several of Lennett's men transplant the fertilised eggs taken from the mice into the artificial wombs. Since the mutiny aboard the colony ship that Bernie had led years earlier, he and his fellow mutineers who had been abandoned on Ra had barely eked out an existence. The scientific knowledge that individual members among them had possessed had not been channelled into the creation of creature comforts, as it well might have been, but into the construction of the wombs and the establishment of the technology for the accelerated growth process that reduced by more than half the time it took a human organism to grow to maturity. The barrenness and spartanlike existence shared by the residents of Ra contrasted sharply with the gleaming metal laboratories they had built.

'I have plans,' Bernie mused, not looking at Shannon but at some inner horizon that brought lights to glitter in the dark pupils of his eyes.

A woman bearing two huge bowls of steaming stew entered the room, set them in front of Shannon and Bernie, and then withdrew.

Shannon stared at the broth and the lumps of matter floating in it. The faintly acrid odour of the stew sickened him.

Across the table, Bernie lifted his bowl in both hands, swallowed hungrily, and put it down. 'I'll soon have enough workers to man the ice mines, workers to filter the stew, workers to turn Ra into something near the Eden you mentioned, Shannon. And then . . .'

Shannon, interested despite his growing eagerness to leave, said, 'And then, Bernie?'

Bernie turned a benign gaze upon Shannon. 'And then we will return to Earth. Oh, with what pomp we shall return!'

Bernie's eyes were no longer benign. The fire of fanaticism now glowed in their muddy centres. 'We shall return with pomp and an army. With weapons, Shannon. We shall right the wrong done to us. Come to think of it, certain anthills do conceal danger. I've heard of a certain species of ant on Earth that can reduce a wild boar — or a man — to nothing but bones in less than an hour.'

'Bernie,' Shannon said, 'the transplantation must be complete by now. I'd like to get going. I'm planning on stopping at Seventh Heaven on the way back to Earth.'

Starson appeared in the doorway. 'The transplantation is complete, Shannon.' His eyes were not on Shannon but on

Bernie, and they were the eyes of the tiger cub who yearns to hunt but whose skill is as yet insufficient.

Bernie roused himself. 'Seventh Heaven? Expensive, that place, or so they tell me. So you'll be wanting your money, Shannon. Naturally. Everything has its price. Everything is for sale to him who will pay. I will pay you for the people you've brought me, and you in turn will pay the ladies of the lanes for their attentions.' He extracted a pouch from beneath his layers of rags and spilled Tokens on the table. 'Count it.'

Shannon did so, and found the sum correct. He nodded to Starson, who came forward and scooped up the Tokens.

'In four months,' Bernie said, 'the artificial wombs will have delivered. In four months, I'll want another shipment.'

Shannon stood up and headed for the door.

'Why do you hesitate, Shannon?' Bernie asked. 'I told you I had plans. Do my plans impinge upon yours?'

Shannon, without turning, said, 'Not at all, Bernie. But my price will be fifteen per cent higher next time.'

Bernie shrugged and held up his hands as if to ward off the very air in the room. 'Who can argue? You're the only supplier of this unusual commodity at the present time. I can't go to a competitor for a better price — not yet, anyway. So fifteen per cent higher the price shall be.'

'What do you mean, you can't go to a competitor yet?' Shannon turned to confront Bernie. 'Do you know something you should tell me?'

Bernie was enjoying his moment. He hunched his shoulders and rolled his eyes. 'Things change all the time. I hear Oxon Kaedler has an eye on your lucrative operation.'

'Who told you that?'

'We heard his ultrafrequency broadcast several days ago. He offered a reward for information about your whereabouts. But don't worry. Would I betray the Mythmaster to a man like Kaedler? I would not.'

Shannon moved swiftly through the door and out into the

long hall. He left the hall and fell into the wild arms of the wind. It tossed him forcefully to one side, and he momentarily lost his balance. Starson, behind him, put out a hand to steady him. The ice was slippery underfoot, and when the wind abated for a moment, Shannon shook himself free of Starson and began to move towards his ship, docked some distance away.

CHAPTER SEVEN

'Come in,' Shannon called out as the hard knock sounded on his cabin door hours after blastoff from Ra.

Starson entered with no smile and no salute.

Shannon looked up from his desk. 'Why so grim? We'll soon be at Seventh Heaven. So smile, man, smile!'

'I've come about Maxevitch.'

'What about Maxevitch?'

'He's dead.'

Shannon leaned forward, gripping the edge of his desk. 'Dead?'

Rawley found him. The meditech says he's been dead for hours.

'Cause of death?'

'Strangulation.'

'Strangulation? Impossible!'

Starson stepped towards the front of the desk and the chair beside it.

'Sit down,' Shannon said, waving him into the chair. 'Now, tell me what—'

'Maxevitch hanged himself. He used a length of computer cable. It not only broke his neck but also sliced through his skin, severing his jugular vein. If he hadn't strangled, he would have bled to death.'

Shannon got up and began to pace back and forth behind his desk. 'Did he leave a note?'

'No. But a note isn't needed to understand why he did it.'

'He was addicted to Mythmakers. He was unstable.'

'Not so unstable as to commit suicide. And his addiction wasn't the cause of his death. You were, Shannon.'

Shannon placed his knuckles on the surface of the desk and leaned over it. 'Explain yourself.'

'You cancelled his quota of Mythmakers,' Starson said quietly. 'You knew he was addicted. You must have known what might happen.'

'I knew that sensory aberrations experienced during withdrawal are only temporary. I knew that a man with guts could tolerate the unpleasantness.'

' "Unpleasantness"? "Agony" would be a more appropriate word.'

Shannon's lips grew white as he pressed them together. When he spoke, his voice was steady, but muscles leaped in his cheeks. 'When it was over, he would have been clean. I did him a favour!'

'You dealt him his death. You said yourself that he was unstable. The aberrations were too much for him to bear. We all heard him moaning in his cabin for days. You could have merely reduced the dosage. Why did you cancel his quota in the first place?'

Shannon sat down. 'One thing should be made clear at this point. I am in command of this ship. I give the orders. You and the other crewmen obey them.'

'You're a simple man, Shannon.'

'Listen to me! I see no reason to subject myself to an examination by you or any other crew member. I told you before that you can sign off this ship as easily as you signed on. But while you're aboard, you are under my command.' He leaned back in his chair. 'I'm sorry about Maxevitch. In many ways he was a good and valuable crewman. But I am not responsible for his death! You might as well say that I am responsible for every man's actions aboard this ship. Utter nonsense, I'm sure you will agree.'

'Command implies a certain commitment to those commanded,' Starson remarked, not taking his gaze from Shannon. 'It isn't enough to simply command. A man in power, if he has any moral sensibility at all or human feeling, must admit that with power goes a responsibility to use that power wisely. You, Shannon, wield the power but care nothing about its results.'

Shannon began to laugh — a deep, unpleasant sound that issued from somewhere deep inside him. 'You talk to me of responsibility and morality! You, Starson! Why, when I hired you, you were nothing but a paid plaything on Level One of Seventh Heaven. Like your former wife, you —'

Starson slammed a fist down on the desk. 'Forget Reba!'

'Like her,' Shannon continued, undaunted, 'you were for sale to any man with enough Tokens and a taste for certain twisted pleasures. So why this intense concern for Maxevitch? You're no saint, Starson. Was he your lover? Is that it?'

Starson's sigh was the breath of despair. 'Shannon, you are, as I said before, a simple man. The feet of simple men crush insects and do not notice. Their fists strike flesh and feel nothing. No, Maxevitch was not my lover. Had he been, you might be able to understand my sorrow over his death. To me Maxevitch was nothing more and nothing less than a human being. As you are.'

Shannon rose, walked around the desk, and stood glaring down at Starson. 'I didn't kill Maxevitch. Maxevitch killed Maxevitch. It's true that I'm a simple man, as you claim. Simple men like me see things and people for what they are. We don't wear rose-coloured glasses to soften our vision of reality, and we don't require Mythmakers to alter it, as do the Maxevitches of this world. We see things as they are, accept them, and act accordingly.'

'Do you see me as I am, Shannon? And, if you do, is what I am sufficient in your simplistic world?'

'Understand one thing, Starson. I hired you because you were the best astrogator I could find willing to sail with me. I have no other use for you. And never forget that you are my astrogator, not my judge and not my jury.'

'Nor you mine, Shannon.'

'There's more than an hour left of your duty tour.'

Starson stood up. 'Maxevitch's record indicate that he requested space burial. The ceremony, such as it will be, is scheduled for nine o'clock tonight.'

'I'll be there.'

Starson went to the door and opened it. Just before he left the cabin, he said, 'I'm sorry, Shannon. For both of us.'

When he was gone, Shannon called his chief engineer on the intercom. When the man responded, Shannon told him that the power reduction was no longer necessary.

'We've been on full power all along,' the chief engineer reminded him in the tone of a plotter. 'You know that, sir.'

'I know that. But announce that tapetexts and other appliances may now be used without restriction.'

'Yes, sir.'

Shannon sat down behind his desk and propped his head in his hands. No tapetext sound would bother Maxevitch now. No song of bird or woman's laugh. The air in the cabin felt oppressive, but Shannon knew that it was not the air that weighed so heavily on his shoulders, causing them to sag. Had he been wrong in disciplining Maxevitch in the way he had chosen? Had Starson's accusation been accurate? No, he knew he was not a murderer. He considered Starson's charge ridiculous. But still his shoulders sagged.

The seductive sensory beams relayed from Seventh Heaven invaded the ship even before the glittering lights of the bordello became visible through the viewplates. The beams plucked at the minds of the men aboard the ship, promising, in sultry tones and words calculated to arouse, joys and delights to match any lusty desire and surpass any — even the most exotic — fantasy.

The beams did what Shannon had failed to do in the days following Maxevitch's death. They put a lilt in the gait of the crewmen and a sparkle in their eyes. The men went about their tasks now with an eagerness that had been noticeably absent during the past several days. They whistled. They exercised. They no longer avoided Shannon's glance, and they answered his questions without the sound of raw anger barely suppressed in their voices.

Shannon too surrendered to the beams, basked in them. 'Ungird your loins,' a female voice whispered, 'and sink into the soft sea of me. Afterwards, I shall anoint you with spices and whisper sweet words in your ear.'

Many two-backed beasts would be born this night, Shannon knew. He roamed through his ship, from empty cargo hold to command cabin. He clapped a crewman on the back in one place, joked with another elsewhere. There was an almost palpable air of anticipation among the men. Sailors everywhere, whether of seas or space, Shannon thought, were essentially the same. They put in at a port and unleashed their raging appetites; and then, upon leaving, they would find their bodies weary, their brains dulled, and their pockets empty. And so they would sail on, the journeys of their lives gaudily spangled with memories of this port, that woman. And when they were old, with neither seas nor stars any longer within their reach, they would sit moodily on Earth or on one of the offworlds and dream dreams of soft flesh and lovely faces and know that, yes, it had all been worthwhile, although so brief, so very brief.

Standing in the command cabin, Shannon requested a probe to determine what other ships were docked at Seventh Heaven. The probe revealed the presence of four other ships. Two freighters under colonial flags, a private pleasure cruiser, and one unidentified ship.

'Space Patrol?' Shannon asked, referring to the unidentified ship, although he doubted that any Patrol ship would sail without identifying digits. Too risky. Such a ship could be disintegrated without warning by the Patrol, without investigation, and without legal complications.

58

'Doubtful, sir,' the crewman at the controls answered. 'It's too big to be a Patroller.'

Shannon briefly considered bypassing Seventh Heaven this time. The presence of the unidentified ship bothered him. But if he gave the order to continue on to Earth, he might well have a mutiny on his hands. The ghost of Maxevitch still haunted the ship. He hoped Seventh Heaven would help to exorcise it. 'Force-field the ship as soon as we dock,' he ordered. 'Set up an electralarm. Starson, come here.'

Starson, who had been sitting quietly at his astrogation panel, looked up. He got up and approached Shannon.

Shannon handed him a tiny metal cylinder. 'Implant this receiver. I'll wear one too. This way, if anyone tries to tamper with the ship while we're here, we'll receive the signals from the electralarm in time.'

Starson took the cylinder and deftly snapped it into place in the surgically created cavity in his right earlobe.

Shannon did the same.

Minutes later, the ship eased itself into the docking area. Except for the on-duty crewmen, the men were already lining up at the lock. Their jokes were loud and bawdy; their eagerness was apparent in their restlessness. When the ship had been secured to Shannon's satisfaction, he announced through the intercom that those wishing to disembark could do so. He added a warning. 'While you take your pleasures — and may they be hearty ones — remember our last visit here and the slogan of the Space Patrol: "The eye that never closes." That's all.'

The men whooped their way through the lock and into Seventh Heaven.

Shannon returned to his cabin, glad of the sudden relative quiet of the ship. It gave him a feeling of peace, and it freed his mind to consider Reba Charlo. As he made ready to join his men, he wondered if Reba would still be an employee of the bordello. Women like Reba came and went, seemingly without reason or plan. Reba might now be in another pleasure palace in another galaxy or star system. She might have vanished forever, as if she had never existed. Perhaps another woman now occupied the seventh level, or perhaps the seventh level was now devoted to activities other than those Shannon had shared with Reba Charlo.

He finished dressing as the sensory beams continued to flash images in his mind that were sometimes wordless, sometimes hotly linear. Feathers and fur and oriental postures flashed through his mind as the beams touched him. Chains. Children with painted bodies, and animals with lurid eyes.

He left his cabin, and then the ship, and stepped into the reception area of Seventh Heaven. He was pleased to see that the damage that had occurred during his last visit had been repaired. A girl was coming towards him. She was not the girl who had greeted him last time, and he began to feel uneasy. If the girl in the reception area could change, then so could the inhabitants of the seven levels. 'Level Seven,' he told the girl before she had a chance to greet him.

'Reba Charlo?'

Shannon nodded, relieved. 'Level Seven. Reba Charlo.'

The girl went to the ornate desk set in a corner of the room and made a notation in the book lying open on its surface. 'The price is . . .'

'I know her price.'

'You will have to wait. Reba is engaged at the moment.'

Shannon felt anger rise to inflame his face. His reaction was not rational, he realised. But somehow he had expected Reba to be at least available to him, if not willing necessarily to welcome him with open arms. 'How long?'

'Reba will let me know when she has completed the services for which she was engaged. We do not schedule encounters here in terms of time. Our employees determine when their services have been satisfactorily rendered. The system makes for satisfied customers. While you wait, may I suggest dalliance on one of the other levels? One might compare such dalliance to an aperitif before a sumptuous banquet. Since you obviously know Reba, you will understand what I mean.'

'I'll wait. I'll use the baths in the meantime. My name is

60

Ackerman. Here's my cashcard. Please call me as soon as Reba is available.'

'Of course, Mr. Ackerman. The baths are just down the corridor. Will you want companionship?'

Shannon gestured impatiently and answered in the negative. He strode down the hall to the gilded door and went through it and into the sim-marble baths.

A husky attendant helped him undress and suggested that he try the large oval bath, which was a blue pool of whirling water.

'You'll find it a most enjoyable sensation, I daresay, sir,' the attendant said. 'We have seeded the water with a species of sea polyp imported from Apollo Prime. I think you will find their behaviour decidedly amusing.

The attendant proceeded to apply a scented oil to Shannon's body, and when he had finished, watched Shannon limp towards the oval bath and stare down into the clear water.

At first Shannon saw nothing. But then, as his eyes became accustomed to the movement of the water, he saw the faintly discernible shapes of the polyps. They were identifiable mainly by their eyes, which appeared as black specks in the blue water. By keeping his gaze on a cluster of the specks, he was able to distinguish the colourless bodies that undulated after and around the eyes.

He sat down on the edge of the pool and eased his lame leg into the warm water. He was about to drop down into the pool when he quickly withdrew his leg, letting out a loud cry of surprise as he did so.

In a matter of seconds the attendant stood beside him. 'The polyps, sir. The touch of their suction centres is a bit of a shock at first. But when you become accustomed to it, as I said, you'll find it all quite amusing.'

Shannon doubted it. But he was not a man to miss any experience. And besides, the attendant was watching him solicitously, and he didn't want to appear foolish. He stood up, and a moment later dived heard-first into the pool.

Under the water, he let out his breath in a sudden rush. He

surfaced. The polyps were all around him. They didn't cling or bite, but they nuzzled his body, and the sensation was not unlike being shocked by a faint current.

'The oil, sir,' the attendant called out. 'It functions as an aphrodisiac for this particular species.'

Shannon lay back and floated face-upwards on the surface of the pool. Beneath him, the polyps discharged their shocking caresses against his bare back and buttocks. The sensation, he decided, was far from unpleasant, once you grew used to it. In fact, it was distinctly pleasurable. He turned over and floated face-down in the water, his eyes open. He tried to capture a polyp, but it eluded his grasp.

The attendant beckoned to him, and he swam to the side of the pool. The attendant held another tiny tube of oil in his hand, and he offered it to Shannon, along with certain sly suggestions. Shannon was about to refuse the oil and the suggestions, but the attendant began to smirk at his hesitation. Shannon accepted the proffered tube and applied the oil to his groin, which the attendant had earlier been too discreet to touch.

He swam back to the centre of the pool, where the water was deepest, and again floated face-down, while the polyps fluttered in a frenzy about his pelvis, abandoning themselves to the ecstasy the oil induced in them.

He turned over in the water like an indolent seal. As he floated on his back, the tumescent part of himself was a fleshy mainmast thrusting above the surface of the water.

The attendant grinned.

Shannon turned over in the water. He raised his head for a breath of air now and then.

Some time later, the attendant had to shout to attract his attention. 'Sir, are you the gentleman who is waiting to visit Level Seven?'

'I am,' Shannon called back. At the same instant, the polyps undid him, and he burst into the water, scattering the colourless beasts and cursing himself and his encounter with them.

He climbed from the pool, and the attendant handed him

an enormous towel. He showered under the sanispray and was given a floor-length robe by the attendant. 'We'll sterilise your clothes, sir, and have them sent up at once to Level Seven.'

'Thank you.'

'After you leave Level Seven,' said the attendant, 'or perhaps during your next sojourn with us, you might like to enjoy yourself with our newest attraction on Level Five. We call it the cupidcat.'

'What's a cupidcat?'

'A mammal from Star System Six, sir.'

'Most amusing, I imagine,' Shannon remarked, as he belted the loose robe about his body.

His sarcasm was either lost on the attendant or deliberately ignored. 'Cupidcats, sir, attempt to mate with any species with whom they come into contact — and they are occasionally successful. Given their sexual proclivities and the fact that they are telekinetic . . . well, the results can be decidedly amusing.'

Shannon handed the man a Token and left the room. He silently condemned both the polyps and himself for what had just happened. But he felt fairly confident that the sight of Reba Charlo — to touch her again — would undo the temporary damage that the polyps had inflicted upon him, which left him limp and sated.

CHAPTER EIGHT

Reba did not rise from her couch as Shannon entered her lavish apartment. She did not lift a hand in greeting, nor raise her voice in welcome. But her fingers moved nervously over the sleek silk covering her chaise, and her eyes were on his. She watched him walk across the room towards her and then abruptly settle himself in a chair draped with velvet.

'Did you have a good journey?' she inquired.

'A profitable one.'

'And now — where?'

'Back to Earth.'

'Home?'

'No, just back to Earth. My home is my ship.'

Reba stretched, raising her arms. Her bracelets tinkled as she did so. 'That is convenient, I should imagine. You travel without ever leaving home. That must make you feel anchored.'

Did it? Her words surprised Shannon. If anything, he had always considered himself a man without anchors. 'You were engaged when I arrived.'

'Did that surprise you?'

'No. But I was disappointed.' At once, he wished he had not spoken. His frank statement would give Reba an advantage over him. He suspected that women like Reba would use any advantage to establish control of situations — and people.

Reba rose and began to remove her bracelets.

'There's no great hurry. We can talk.'

'As you wish.' She drew up a chair and sat down beside him. 'How old are you, Shannon?'

'Why do you ask?'

'The very young men who come here often want to talk for a time. They ask me questions. They want to know why I am here. They ask me if I am ever lonely. They are so nervous, those boys.'

Shannon ignored the implied jibe. 'Are you ever lonely?'

Bluntly: 'Always.'

'Even when you . . . ?'

'Yes, even then. Now, you must ask me, as those boys do, why I do not leave this place and go . . .' She waved her arms in the air. 'Oh . . . away.'

'I assume it is because you like it here. You must, or you would not be here.'

'You endorse the doctrine of free will, then?'

'Certainly.'

'And yet you are the Mythmaster who murders free will in your victims.'

'That's different. Mythmadness is not a normal condition, as you should remember.'

'I remember.' Her expression darkened. 'Can you conceive of states of mind other than that of Mythmadness which leave a person no real room for choice? Can you understand that many people do what they do because they must do it?'

Shannon found her statements cryptic. Was she saying that she had no choice but to remain in Seventh Heaven? He could not believe that. Since he had spent his life choosing his destiny and making his decisions, he believed that everyone else who was not a weakling or an idiot did the same. He changed the subject. 'Have you been here long?'

'All my life.'

He protested that he had never seen her on his previous visits, with the exception of the last one.

'Seventh Heaven is a state of mind,' she told him. 'It is the place where people come together and wind themselves around and within one another and try to feel what they call love but settle for mere physical contact. Contact without commitment. Yes, Seventh Heaven is a state of mind.'

'I see.'

Reba allowed herself the briefest of smiles. 'No, you don't see. I meant that Seventh Heaven is the closest I can come to realising the state of mind that I experienced once with ... with Starson. He was the first, you know.'

'You loved him?'

'I love him.' Reba got up and gazed out the window through which stars spilled their light. 'Or say simply, if you prefer, that I made contact with him. You might feel more comfortable thinking of it in that way.' She turned her back to the window, obliterating the stars. 'Why do you come to

65

Seventh Heaven, Shannon?' Without waiting for an answer, she went on. 'You come — correct me if I err — to lose yourself, not to find someone. That is why you were angered last time. Because I was about to reach out to you, and you sensed it and made yourself unreachable. Your anger towards me was a way of keeping a distance between us. Having understood that, I accepted it. It is often that way with the men who come here. On every level, it is the same.'

'You made me hate you.'

'Yes. Yes, I did. But only when I realised that you needed to. That would make matters right for you. It would make you feel alone and free — a condition I suspect you equate with safety, if not with joy.'

'Enough, Reba.'

'No, Shannon, it is true. I endangered you by being so open at first.'

'I don't hate you.'

Reba crossed the room, her eyes deeply ambered, her gait steady but somewhat stiff. When she stood in front of Shannon, she held out her hands to him, and he saw that the woman who had been speaking to him had vanished. Now, the curve of Reba's lips and the upthrust promise of her breasts told the story of another woman, one well-bastioned and practised in the art of — what had she called it? — *contact.*

He let her draw him up to stand in front of her. He obligingly held out his arms, and she unfastened his robe and slipped it from his shoulders. She looked down at him. And then up again at his face.

'Conversation,' she said, 'sometimes kills desire.'

'No, I was in the baths before coming up here. There's a species of — '

'Sea polyp!' she cried, her eyes brightening. 'So that's my competition!'

'You were engaged when I arrived,' Shannon blustered.

'Can you ever forgive me?' She put her hands on his hips and stepped backwards.

Shannon let himself be led into the adjoining room. Reba

66

ignored his limp, but her body moved in such a way that she did not in any way accent it or impede his unnatural rolling gait. She pointed to the bed beneath the canopy of mirrors, and he lay down upon it. His nakedness made him feel vulnerable. He damned the polyps, and himself as well for dallying with the bizarre little beasts!

Reba touched a panel on the wall, and the room glowed with subdued flashes of colour. The colours caressed her skin as she freed herself of her gown and sat down on the edge of the bed.

'Listen,' she said, 'to the colours.'

After several minutes, Shannon was able to distinguish the sounds that were the various hues. Softly fluted — the blues. Drumming reds. Yellows like shrieking brass. 'How . . . ?'

'The spectrum is transmitted through a sound disassembler, and the console computer over there translates the light frequencies into harmonic variations.'

He opened his mouth to say something, but Reba lay down beside him, pressing an index finger to her lips, and he saw the gesture reflected in the mirrors overhead. As she raised herself on one elbow, he watched the other Reba in the mirrored sky. It was some time before he recognised the words she was whispering in his ear.

'I hate you, I hate you!'

Something stirred within him. The Reba of the mirrored sky now shielded his own body from his sight. She was still repeating her soft litany, and somehow it helped repair the depredations the polyps had inflicted upon it. He put his arms around her and pressed her shoulders down. When he was above her, his lame leg sought to open the ravine of her thighs and encountered no resistance.

Reba had stopped speaking, but her body, in its own language, repeated the message she had been transmitting. She began to fight him. Her fingernails bloodied his shoulderblades.

As the colours continued to chorus in the room, the mirrors overhead recorded the warriors and the battlefield.

When it was over at last, Shannon withdrew from her and

lay back in the bed. He stretched and sighed and knew himself the victor. But then he began to remember Reba's earlier words and entertain the suspicion that her behaviour had been made to order so that he would feel himself to be the conqueror, and the battle well-waged and surely won. But, he now admitted to himself, he had been expecting her to fight him off. Why? He could not say. Perhaps she had sensed his expectations and obliged him, since it was her task to please. Her performance, if that's what it had been, had been perfect — flawless. It had made him feel the master of the situation and of her. She had provided undeniably exquisite service. She had sold; he had bought. Their bargain was now consummated. He should feel pleased. But he did not. He felt oddly denied.

They lay side by side for several minutes without touching, neither of them speaking, both of them avoiding their reflections in the mirrors. The music coloured the room.

Reba at last added her own notes to the score being played by the console computer. 'Starson told me that he had heard that you were once a member of the Spacelane Five Fleet.'

'I was.'

'Now you are not. Why not?'

It was an old story that no longer aroused much bitterness in Shannon. But he did not want to tell it to Reba. Not now, not here. 'That was a long time ago.'

Reba persisted. Something about the tone of her voice convinced Shannon that she really wanted to know. He began to tell her, and in the telling, to remember another Shannon who was almost a complete stranger to him now.

'I was raised in one of the communal nurseries on Earth under the care of a mother surrogate. You spoke before about anchors. Well, I had no anchor. No parents who would admit to me. Nothing and no one. But I didn't mind, because I eventually began to see my status as a way of being totally free. When I came to the end of my term, I qualified for the Space Academy. I got my first ship when I was only twenty. By the time I was twenty-four, I held the rank of executive officer. It was during a routine shuttle run to the Moon colony that my career, which had been developing so auspiciously, ended.

'What happened?'

'We altered course to avoid a meteorite swarm, and suddenly found ourselves headed towards a cluster of the orbiting solitary cells launched by the Space Patrol.

'They were empty?'

'No, our biodata indicated that each one contained a prisoner. About the same time, we discovered that the meteorite swarm had split into two broad bands bordering us. If we maintained our altered course, chances were that we would pass harmlessly through the path left by the swarm.'

'What about the solitary cells?'

'Yes, the cells. Well, they were dead ahead and travelling at a much slower rate than we were. Our commander rejected my suggestion that we alter course to avoid warping them out of their programmed orbits and into the meteorite bands. He pointed out — correctly — that if we altered course, we would risk serious damage from the meteorites. I reminded him that the cells contained prisoners, and he in turn reminded me that such prisoners had no legal status and, in fact, no real identity any longer under Patrol law. Their loss, if loss there should prove to be, he said, would be unfortunate, but not punishable, and not damaging to his academy record. I guess I argued rather heatedly. Later, at my trial, the prosecutor claimed I had acted "rashly and in a manner clearly mutinous". The charge was valid, because I took it upon myself to alter our course in order to avoid destroying the cells. By so doing, I assumed command of the ship and countermanded orders, however briefly and for whatever purpose. And that is mutiny.'

'Did the prisoners survive?'

'No. I acted too late. They were destroyed by the meteorites. Our ship also sustained considerable damage as a result of what I had done. I was later discharged from Five Fleet with forfeiture of pay and tarnished honour.'

'Honour.' Reba seemed to taste the word. 'Our lives are

bounded by words. Our behaviour is corrupted by them. Instead of silver spoons, words are put in our mouths practically at birth, and we spend the rest of our lives gagging on them. Honour. Loyalty. Love. No wonder we never find out who we really are.'

'I know who I am. I'm not the former executive officer of the Spacelane Five Fleet. That was another man I once met and have since forgotten. I'm not the Mythmaster, either. He's a creation of the Fastfax. I am simply a man who makes his own words and his own meanings and doesn't give a damn any more for orbiting solitary cells or the Space Patrol or any properly charted routes on prescribed trails. I make my own life now, and if it isn't beyond reproach, it is at least all mine.'

'You are also a liar, Shannon.'

He turned to stare at her. She met his gaze, her face solemn.

'A liar,' she repeated. 'You're a liar, because the man you once were is not a stranger to you. You tried to avoid killing those prisoners, and you failed. But the fact that you tried is something you obviously still live with. You lie to yourself, Shannon, as we all do.'

He smiled wryly and touched her cheek. He let his hand encircle the white column of her throat. 'You may be right. It may be that we have to lie to ourselves in order to survive.'

'We lie to one another for the same reason.'

'You're right. How right you are! Think of the wars Earth has waged in the last century — wars without number. They were fought, or so our leaders said, to protect a burgeoning nation or to preserve our sacred traditions. Or to maintain territorial rights. Only the generals and the munitions manufacturers and the men who sold oil or built banks really knew why those wars were fought. For profit.

'I remember the prosecutor's summation at my trial. He called me a dangerous man who should not be allowed to assume responsibility in the spacelanes. Now, I'm not so bitter any more, but consider that statement for a moment. Words again, you see. I thought I was responsible for the

lives of those legal nonentities, those prisoners in their solitary cells. And my commander thought he was responsible
for avoiding the risk of damage to his ship, his men, and his
reputation. We were, of course, both right. And the prosecutor had his own ideas about responsibility. He was after
an appointment to the Council of Nonterrestrial Law, a legal
and political plum well worth possessing. The trial, he knew,
would get him noticed. A conviction might net him a new
title. NTL counsellor.'

'NTL counsellor,' Reba mused. 'More words. Words are the
chains we drag around with us all our lives, and they won't let
us *live!*' She started to rise from the bed when a sudden
silence screamed in the room. The music from the console
computer had died in mid-phrase. Its colours had vanished.

CHAPTER NINE

A figure stood in the doorway of the bedroom. It was obese
and no more than four feet tall. It wore a ballooning garment
of some soft material, above which its hairless head bobbed
like a giant egg.

'Get out!' Reba commanded. 'You have no right on Level
Seven while I am engaged.'

The figure's body jiggled, its black eyes remained steady,
its claws flexed at the end of its short arms.

'Oxon Kaedler comes. Demands audience with woman,
Reba, and man, Shannon. At once!'

Both Shannon and Reba had heard the words although the
creature's mouth had not opened.

'Shannon,' Reba whispered. 'What . . . ?'

'It's a neomorph. Class seven from Darien's secondary star

71

system. Home world, Caliban. They're telepathic, the Calibaneers.'

'Get out!' Reba cried. She reached up, extracted a colourless capsule from a receptacle above the bed, and promptly swallowed it. Within seconds, the capsule altered the cellular structure of her skin so that it refracted light. To anyone looking at her, she appeared to be fragmented, each fragment a different colour. The capsules served those who used them as both a means of ornament and a way of achieving personal privacy.

The Calibaneer remained motionless. 'Kaedler comes! Kaedler coming!'

Shannon sprang from the bed and sprinted past the neomorph in the other room. He retrieved his robe from the floor, where Reba had dropped it, and hurriedly put it on.

The Calibaneer loped past him towards the outer door with surprising speed, considering the large amount of flesh smothering his skeletal structure. He clawed open the outer door. 'Kaedler comes. Kaedler soon here.'

Shannon heard the creature's words echoing in his mind as Reba appeared beside him. Both of them stared at the open door through which the Calibaneer had disappeared. Before either of them had a chance to speak, the creature returned, a thin tubular device clutched in one claw. The device emitted a pulsing beam of light that guided the apparatus that moved through the door and into the apartment.

'This Kaedler,' the Calibaneer announced.

The apparatus consisted of little more than a circle of gleaming metal about three feet in diameter that hovered only inches above the floor. Its upper surface was perforated in a number of places. The startling thing about the metal disc was not its gliding sibilance or odd construction, but the figure that hovered in the air above it. Two feet above the surface of the disk lolled a naked man. He rolled in the air, turned, and turned again. At times he was facing the disc beneath him. At other times, he lay spread-eagled above it with no visible means of support. His skin was a mottled brown in which patches of a raw pinkness showed. He wore no rings or other ornaments.

'This Kaedler,' announced the Calibaneer, pointing at the nude man. 'Burned, he. Vocal structure voided. He tell you his talk through me.' The creature fell silent, seeming to listen. Then, almost gaily, 'The dead man salutes the living one and the woman. His words following.' The Calibaneer's eyelids lowered. He seemed to be entering a trance state. When he spoke again, his lips moved. He was no longer communicating telepathically, except with Oxon Kaedler.

Reba and Shannon listened to the voice that was not Kaedler's but the neomorph's. They heard the speech Kaedler delivered to them through the Calibaneer, who was transmitting his thoughts.

'What they told me about you, Reba Charlo, is so delightfully true! You are indeed the most delectable merchandise for sale here on any level. And you, John Shannon. So we meet at last! I would shake hands, but, as you can see, my body is no longer suited for such contact. I suffered severe burns in the fire, and even now I still feel those flames burning beneath my skin. My voice is gone. Hence, my need of the neomorph and its telepathic powers. Now, you must have questions to ask me. I am full of answers. Begin.'

Shannon shook his head as if to clear it of the grotesque vision confronting him. 'How does that thing support you?'

'Air is vented up through its base. The air is humidified, lubricated, sterilised, and sufficiently supportive. You see, I cannot be touched, nor can I bear to touch. Despite the fact of the many skin grafts I suffered at the hands of the meditechs, I burn still from the fire.'

'What fire?'

'An accident in my villa on Venus. The solar stream that negated the excess moisture in the atmosphere went out of phase one day. Ha! "Berserk" would be a better word. The room in which I was sleeping became a furnace. Imagine sheets of fire, gobbets of it! Imagine the pure pain, Shannon!'

'I heard reports of your death.'

'I am and have always been an enterprising man, as you may know.'

'I know. All the worlds know it.'

'In years past, I had numerous threats made on my life. In fact, I suspect that someone in my employ tampered with the solar stream, thus causing the fire that nearly killed me. There are those who would have sought my death for reasons of their own. But I had prepared for just such an event. And when it occurred, I merely exploited it. The Oxon Kaedler who died in the fire was a clone. I had arranged for the creation of that clone from my cellular structure years earlier. You, Shannon, as Mythmaster, are undoubtedly familiar with the technique.'

'I am. Take a cell from any part of a person's body. Said cell contains a complete set of chromosomes to determine the genetic inheritance of that person. Implant that cell nucleus in a female egg in which you have destroyed the nucleus, and then implant the egg in a womb and let it grow. The result is — '

'A carbon copy of the owner of the original cell nucleus! Just so! My copy — the clone — died. I live! The clone had been aged in accelerative sequence to resemble me. The authorities, ever efficient, ran a genetic tracetest and were satisfied that I was indeed dead. The courts then so declared me. In effect, they gave me a greater freedom than I have ever previously known. Now my various enterprises can prosper without interference from the Space Patrol or other legal organisations. I cannot be accused, nor tried, nor convicted, because Oxon Kaedler, according to the sacred records of the courts on Earth, is dead. And no one can prosecute a dead man!'

'They'll find a way eventually.'

'Perhaps. Maybe someday. Meanwhile . . .' The voice trailed away provocatively.

Shannon's thoughts raced. The Calibaneer had sought him out, and Reba as well. Kaedler was here for no idle purpose. He needed time to think, to plan strategies for any and every conceivable eventuality. 'How did you know I was here?' he asked Kaedler.

Kaedler assumed a sitting position. He raised his arms and spread his legs. 'I pay many people for many services. Your recent client —'

'Bernie Lennet!' Shannon exclaimed, anticipating Kaedler's announcement.

'The same. He and I have talked of the possibility of doing business together. He contacted me after your recent departure from Ra and told me that you had said you were planning to visit Seventh Heaven on your way back to Earth. So I came here to talk with you. My unidentified ship is docked here. For a man of your intelligence, Shannon, you tend to talk entirely too much, and to the wrong people.'

'What do you want with me?'

'Now we come to it.' Kaedler let himself fall forward, to sprawl more comfortably on his air stream. His eyes were on Reba, but he spoke to Shannon. 'I want to buy a partnership in your business, Shannon. I also want to buy your body. I will pay well and at once for both.'

'I can understand your wanting my business, but not my body. Explain yourself.'

The Calibaneer's eyelids flickered as Kaedler's next words emerged from its mouth. 'There is a growing market for flesh throughout the galaxies, as you well know. Your methods of supplying that market are both direct and economical. I want to expand the market and do the supplying. I want to be your partner, Shannon. I am perfectly willing for you to continue supervising the operation as Mythmaster.

'As for your body, no, I am not speaking of lust. But look at me. What good is this burned-out hull that houses me? It is a hindrance to me. Let me buy a single cell from you, Shannon. Perhaps from your noble heart — and I shall then clone it and age it and implant my own genetic code upon it. Certain elements of that code, at any rate. Not all, since I want to retain your magnificent physical structure.'

'I think I see what you have in mind, Kaedler. Correct me if I'm wrong. Oxon Kaedler is legally dead. If Oxon Kaedler were to inhabit a cloned body outwardly resembling John Shannon, and if that Kaedler-Shannon were then to arrange for the demise of the original and legitimate Shannon — why, then Kaedler would be even safer than he is at present, because he could effectively take over the life of the "dead" John Shannon. The answer, Kaedler, is no.'

A sigh slid between the Calibaneer's lips. 'Reba Charlo,' Kaedler said through the Calibaneer, 'you are a woman of some sense, I have been told. You take today and let tomorrow go. Tell your companion that he is being foolish. Tell him I will pay one million Tokens for a partnership in his business, and an additional million for one cell from his body. Tell him to be wise.'

Reba remained silent for a moment; and then: 'Shannon needs no telling. He is his own man. No woman can control such a man.'

'Reba Charlo could control such a man,' came Kaedler's sly reply.

'And what about me?' Reba inquired, ignoring Kaedler's crude compliment. 'Your neomorph said you wanted to see me as well as Shannon.'

'Yes, I did. I am badly injured, as you can observe. Until I can, shall we say, reconstitute myself in a more fitting manner and mould. I must take my pleasures in whatever limited ways are available to me. You, Reba, know much about pleasure. You could help to end my loneliness and make me once again able to experience wounds from the arrows of Eros.'

Reba's face darkened in distaste. Her lips grew taut.

'Don't look at me like that!' Kaedler screamed, causing the body of the Calibaneer to shudder. 'Stop it at once! I don't demand direct ministrations. I cannot tolerate the pain. But I would like to watch you and your companions at your love play. I might offer an occasional suggestion. Then too, with some training, I am sure you could learn to manipulate the air vents beneath me in a manner that would give me some brief delight. You see, even in my deplorable condition, certain possibilities of pleasure still remain available to me. And

76

later, when I am cloned in the shape of Shannon here, you will find me rewarding.'

Reba turned away.

'Five hundred thousand Tokens plus an annual retainer,' Kaedler whispered.

'I am not worth it,' Reba said.

'Oh, my dear, you are, you truly are! Is it agreed, then?'

'No, it is not agreed. I will remain here in Seventh Heaven.'

'Ah, the point, the very point, my dear Reba. Seventh Heaven and you. I own the one now; I covet the other.'

'*You* own Seventh Heaven?' Reba exclaimed.

'I have just arranged to become its owner, yes. I'm sure I shall find it a lucrative and amusing sideline to my more boring pursuits. Unfortunately, the staff could not be included in the arrangements. Well, Reba?'

'No, Kaedler.'

The Calibaneer's body shook as Kaedler's rage stormed through it. 'You say no? You *dare* to? To *me*? Know this, Reba Charlo. You will agree to my offer, or you will have no choice but to agree to other, less attractive offers which I shall quickly arrange with visitors yet to come to Seventh Heaven. I'll soon turn your heaven into an endless hell! So consider carefully, Charlo!'

'No.'

'Is it the money? You want more money?'

Reba laughed. 'It is not the money. But I belong to no man and to every man. But I will not belong to you, Kaedler.'

'Shannon!' Kaedler shouted. 'What of you?'

Shannon didn't hesitate. Although Kaedler's offer was an intriguing one, he was fairly certain that he could play Kaedler's game and play it better than Kaedler could. In fact, he was sure it would be a pleasure to try. A surge of perversity welled within and made him smile as he watched Kaedler's body roll in agitation on its invisible columns of air. 'Like Reba,' he said quietly, 'I make my own choices, and there are some things — a few — I will not do.'

'Surely you do not consider yourself a moral man, Shannon?'

Shannon shook his head, his smile broadening. 'Not at all. But the thought of a mind like yours in a body like mine makes me retch. Besides, Kaedler, I enjoy competition. So your business deal has no appeal for me either. My answer, like Reba's, is no.'

'I buy!' Kaedler shrilled. 'I sell! Day after day, year in and year out. I will double my offer to both of you. Well?'

Neither Shannon nor Reba responded.

Kaedler's voice, when it came through the lips of the Calibaneer a moment later, contained the furred sound of the hunting tarantula. 'No one thwarts Oxon Kaedler. What he cannot buy, he takes, or he destroys it! He will take you both — or worse!'

The Calibaneer's eyes burst open as his mouth abruptly closed. Obviously following Kaedler's instructions, he guided the apparatus and the now-silent man suspended above it to a corner of the room.

Shannon felt the impending danger, although he could not yet perceive its form. 'Is there a way out of here other than through that door?' he asked Reba in a whisper.

But she was already heading towards the open door. Before Shannon could move to stop her, the Calibaneer stepped in front of her and swung a claw up and then down in a deadly arc. Reba leaped backward, out of its path, and collided with Shannon, who had hurried to her side to draw her away from the grinning neomorph. 'There's a way,' she whispered. 'The bedroom.' She began to race towards it.

Shannon ran after her. At the door, he glanced over his shoulder and caught a glimpse of Kaedler motioning wildly to the hordes of neomorphs who were tumbling through the door and heading towards the bedroom. Before he could slam the door on them, one of the neomorphs managed to get inside the bedroom. He cried out in pain as the creature's claws embedded themselves in the flesh of his leg. He shook his leg violently in an attempt to free himself, and cried out again in pain and fury.

At the same moment, Reba palmed a panel in the wall, which swung open to reveal a tunnel slanting downwards. Shannon's cry whirled her around. She saw him succeed in closing the door and locking it. She moved swiftly to a button barely visible on the wall and pressed it, flattening herself against the wall as she did so.

There was a faint whir, as of distant wings, and within seconds mirrored panels set at odd angles against one another sprang up from the floor to the ceiling. Five Rebas stood reflected in them. The five moved and became nine. As Reba fled through the mirrored maze she had long ago memorised, which was often used for the purpose of adding spice to waning pleasure, the nine Rebas multiplied, all running with her. She reached Shannon, who was battling the neomorph. Blood flowed from his wound, bathing both the floor and the creature clinging to him.

'This way!' she cried. As she shouted the words, she seized the jewelled pendant that hung around her neck and opened it. She removed the tiny instrument inside and pointed it at the neomorph. A flash of light struck the creature.

'Shannon!' she cried, holding out her hand to him.

He limped towards her, grimacing, and took her hand.

'It will be sedated in seconds,' she said, referring to the neomorph. 'Hurry!'

As she guided Shannon through the intricacies of the mirror maze, the neomorph loosened its grip and thudded to the floor.

They turned, moved forward, and then seemed to circle back again. The mirrors were ripe with Shannons and Rebas.

'There!' Reba exclaimed, pointing to the tunnel.

Shannon came up to it and looked down into the pool of clear water far below.

'It's usually used for bathing — afterwards,' Reba said. 'But it can also be used as a way of escape, if we're lucky.' She eased herself up into the mouth of the tunnel and slid down it.

Shannon quickly followed her. As he hit the water, he saw

that Reba was already swimming towards the shallow end of the pool. He swam after her, bloodying the water behind him.

They emerged from the pool at the same moment. Reba paused to bend the stalk of an artificial flower.

'What . . . ?'

'It will sound the alarm,' Reba responded as she flung her wet hair back from her face. 'It will alert your crew. You'll have time to get to your ship. Through here.'

She opened the door that had been hidden within the design of a painting that covered one entire wall.

Shannon passed through the door and paused only long enough to tear a piece of cloth from his robe and tie it as a tourniquet around his thigh.

'The lift is down there at the end of the hall,' Reba told him.

Shannon headed towards it, and then suddenly stopped. He turned back, to find Reba standing motionless in the open doorway. 'Come on!' he shouted to her.

She took a step towards him and then halted.

He limped back to where she stood and held out a hand. 'Kaedler will have his way with you if you stay.'

'Many other men have.'

'I doubt it. I believe that none have known you. I know that I have not. Now, come with me!'

'With you?'

'I want you to have a chance to choose what you want to do once we get out of here. Kaedler offers you no choice.'

'You'd better hurry.'

Shannon snorted in anger and began to limp back down the long hall. He wanted to look back, to call out to Reba, but he stifled the impulse. When he reached the end of the hall, he pressed the palm of his hand against the lever to summon the lift. It came within seconds. He got in.

Reba, looking small and distant, still stood alone at the far end of the hall.

The lift doors began to whisper shut. Shannon slammed his

hands against them and stood in the opening. 'Reba! I'm not asking you to choose me! But reject Kaedler!'

Reba glanced behind her and then began to move slowly towards Shannon. She began to run. As she stooped beneath his outstretched arms and entered the lift, the red warning light set in the ceiling ruddied her pale face.

'Is there any way to contact my men?' Shannon asked her.

'You can use the intercom there.'

He spoke into the receptor set in the wall, which Reba had showed him. 'Shannon here. All crewmen report back to the ship at once. Repeat. At *once!*'

A moment later Starson's voice came through the receptor. 'What's wrong, Shannon?'

'Oxon Kaedler. Get yourself and the men back to the ship.'

Starson's expletives were colourful. Then, with a groan, 'Yes, sir.'

CHAPTER TEN

As Shannon and Reba came out of the lift on the lowest level and began to race across the broad expanse of the reception area, the girl who had greeted Shannon when he arrived earlier stopped them, her face pale.

'Reba!' she cried. 'Did you see Oxon Kaedler? He . . .'

'I saw him, Lenore.'

'He claimed he owned Seventh Heaven. He had a contract to prove it. He insisted upon going up to Level Seven. I couldn't stop him. Reba, where are you going?'

Kaedler's voice suddenly shrilled through the audiation system, silencing Lenore.

'Close all exits. I want the man Shannon and the woman Charlo held!'

Lenore, alarmed, whispered, 'What did you do to him?'

'Refused him,' Reba replied. 'Good-bye, Lenore.'

Shannon and Reba entered the dock site and found Starson standing tensely beside the ship's open lock sphincter. When he saw them coming, he moved forward to meet them. 'Reba,' he said in surprise. 'What are you doing here?'

'Never mind that,' Shannon muttered. 'What about the crew?'

'All aboard. What the hell's going on? Will somebody tell me?'

Reba moved through the Sphincter.

Starson called after her, 'Where do you think you're going?'

She didn't respond.

Shannon said, 'Kaedler made her an offer which she found unsatisfactory. So she's coming back to Earth with us.'

Starson studied Shannon's face. 'With us? Or with you?'

'None of your business. Reba's none of your business now. Neither am I. Get aboard.'

'Reba Charlo!'

It was Kaedler's voice booming through the empty reception area from the invisible audiation system. 'I give you one last opportunity to remain with me. And a warning. If you leave me now, I shall hunt you down wherever you go, herd you on, and ultimately destroy you. There will be no resting place for you. No haven in all the worlds. I will see to it that the planets close their doors to you. The stars will show you no light. Consider carefully, Charlo! And you too, Shannon. The same fate awaits you, I guarantee it!'

Shannon stepped through the lock sphincter and beckoned to Starson, who entered behind him and then sealed the lock.

'You'll have to take the ship up,' Shannon said to Starson. 'Set course for Earth. Kaedler's ship is in the docking area. It's the one without identifying digits. Disable it.' He placed his arm on Reba's shoulder, and the two of them moved slowly down the corridor in the direction of Shannon's cabin. A moment later, half-turning, Shannon called back to Starson, 'Reduce acceleration during lift-off by point-nine-nine. I won't have time for medical treatment before lift-off, and normal acceleration will cause additional blood loss.'

Starson turned and headed for the command cabin.

When Shannon reached his cabin with Reba's help, he limped at once to the viewplate and looked out, waiting. Ninety seconds later he saw what he had been waiting to see — the thin needle of light that burst part of the plating on Kaedler's ship and dissolved it, leaving a gaping hole just to the rear of the fin section. He strapped himself into an acceleration couch and ordered Reba to do the same.

After liftoff, he released the spongy bands binding him to the couch and stood up gingerly.

Reba remained on her couch, staring upward at nothing. 'We're away?'

'We're away.' He punched the code sequence to summon medical aid into the callboard. Sterile suction cups began to scour the bloodstains from the couch.

He limped to his desk and sat down, easing his injured leg out in front of him. 'Your spectral capsule is wearing off,' he reminded Reba. 'You'll need clothes unless you have more capsules.'

'I have no more.'

'You'll find crew coveralls in the locker over there. They'll have to do until we arrive Earthside.'

As Reba released the bands binding her to the couch and stood up, Shannon bent forward and loosened the tourniquet he had tied around his leg. He waited a moment, and then retied it, glancing up at Reba. He became aware of the difference in her movements. Now, as she searched among his clothes hanging from the racks of the locker, her movements were no longer indolent, as they had been on Level Seven, but quick and sharp. Something about her had altered subtly; something within her had changed. He sensed it. He felt an uneasiness that bordered on discomfort. The woman facing the open locker was a stranger to him — here. It did not matter that he knew her name and had known the rich secrets of her body. That was in another time, another place. The game might still be played between them, but they would have to learn new rules, because this was elsewhere and another age.

Shannon's musing ended as Reba slipped into a pair of coveralls and zipped them up to her throat. She freed her hair from beneath the low collar and bent forward to roll up the cuffs that puddled about her feet. 'Grey is not my colour,' she observed wryly as she caught a glimpse of herself in Shannon's mirror.

'You'll need shoes. Try those flight slippers there.'

She slid her feet into the soft slippers that belonged to Shannon, and rolled up her sleeves. 'You'd better change too,' she said. 'That robe is soaking wet.'

He nodded as a knock sounded on the door. 'Come!'

The meditech who entered tried to hide his surprise at the sight of Reba, but failed to do so.

'My leg,' Shannon said.

The meditech bent down and opened the small kit he carried and then carefully examined the wound. He plunged a hypodermic into Shannon's thigh. He swabbed the wound and then skilfully glazed it with a translucent paste of dermiseptic. 'Here,' he said, handing Shannon a bottle of blue capsules. 'Two a day, morning and night.'

Shannon nodded his thanks and his dismissal, and the meditech, with a glance in Reba's direction, left the cabin.

'There's an empty cabin next door,' Shannon told Reba. 'You can use it. We'll be Earthside in six days. If there's anything you need . . .'

'I'll ask Starson.'

'You'll ask me. Starson is the astrogator of this ship. I'm its commander.'

A flicker of fury blazed in Reba's eyes, and was quickly extinguished. 'As you say.'

'I suggest that you confine yourself to your cabin as much as possible during the trip. Your presence could very well prove to be a disruptive influence among the crew, and I would prefer not to encourage such disruption. As I said, we'll be Earthside in six days, and then you will be free to do as you please.'

'Free, Shannon? We talked earlier, you and I, about freedom.'

'We did.'

'I will be "free", as you put it, to reregister with Central Census and have a duplicate licence issued to me so that I can seek employment elsewhere. You know, of course, that all people in my profession are legally licensed.'

'Yes. But you could register in some other category if you so chose.'

'Could I?' Reba almost smiled. 'I know nothing about computer technology. I cannot claim any knowledge of the world of business. Correction. Not knowledge applicable in either Earth or offworld commerce as the term is usually understood. What else am I to do, "free" though I am?'

'Kaedler threatened to hunt us down. It's something you should think about.'

'Men like Oxon Kaedler thrive on threats. He will have forgotten me already.'

'Perhaps.' Shannon didn't think that Kaedler would have forgotten Reba. First of all, she was not an easily forgotten woman, and secondly, she had both taunted and refused him. As he himself had done. Men like Kaedler, Shannon was certain, did not take either taunts or refusals with resigned shrugs or lapses of memory. 'I'll show you where your cabin it.'

Reba shook her head. 'I'll find it. You said it was the one next door?'

'To the right as you enter the corridor.'

At the door, Reba turned and said, 'Will I see you during the rest of the trip?'

'Of course.'

She disappeared.

What had she said as she left? Shannon asked himself. Or had she said anything at all? Shannon thought she had said something that sounded like 'Seventh Heaven'. It had sounded like a question. But perhaps he had imagined it. He knew that the mind sometimes heard only what it wanted to hear, and if what it wanted to hear had not been spoken, why, then the mind would manufacture the unspoken words to soothe the deluded hearer. He was suddenly furious with himself and with Reba. Why had he insisted upon bringing her aboard? She could have handled Kaedler, given time. He knew it, and he believed Reba knew it, too. But he had practically pleaded with her to accompany him. Well, not pleaded exactly. But he'd been damned persuasive. Why? He knew why. Because a war had been declared between himself and Reba. A war that would be fought with thoughts and desires but no single physical weapon. But if that were indeed the case, why had she surrendered at last and come with him? Didn't she realize that wars left wounds? Or had she really surrendered? She might need the war as much as he did. He swung awkwardly around in his chair, and as he did so, his leg hit the side of the desk. He cried out in pain and cursed, not himself but Reba.

Maxevitch was no longer the only ghost who haunted the ship in the days following their departure from Seventh Heaven. Reba seemed to be everywhere. Shannon would find her sitting in the crew's mess sipping juice and stroking the cook's civet cats. Or he would come upon her in a corridor, and she would ask if they were on schedule, and he would tell her that, yes, they were. Once he visited Starson's cabin on ship's business, and he found her there. Another time, he noticed her with Starson in the cargo hold.

It was not that she disobeyed his order to remain in her cabin. The times when she left it were few, and he had not imposed a rigid quarantine. Was he, then, seeking her?

He found himself expecting to see her where he knew she would not be — in the stores locker, in the crew's exercise area, everywhere. She haunted both the ship and himself. Finally, although he had fought the impulse for days, he switched on the telepanel and dialled her cabin. She was there, wearing the grey coveralls and flat slippers he had given her. She sat in a chair with her head thrown back and her eyes closed. Her hands rested limply in her lap. He noticed that she had tied back her hair with a piece of pink plastene that she had evidently taken from one of the cook's mechmeal containers.

As he stared at her, he saw opulence. He saw the opulence that had surrounded her on Level Seven and of which she was a definite part. Beneath her grey coveralls, he saw the sleek flesh that he had touched, and still watching and imagining and still haunted by her, he heard her soft cries that had been born during their union, and tasted again the hot juices of her mouth and thighs. He felt his skin grow cold and then hot again as he imagined himself sinking down upon her and speaking with joy her name, something he had never allowed himself to do. Something he could not do.

He switched off the telepanel and turned on his tapetext, but neither action exorcised the ghost whose name was not Maxevitch.

On the day they were due Earthside, Shannon spent the last few hours before the setdown in his command cabin. He supervised the transmission of false flight data and received clearance from Northstates Control. He checked each member of the crew to be sure that they had their forged identity papers. He sent one of the crewmen into the cargo hold to seal off the cubicles that had held the mice. Another man was dispatched to laser identifying digits on the outer hull of the ship.

An hour before landing, Shannon was in his own cabin, glancing over documents and making notes for his next foray after contraband.

He opened the door in response to a knock and admitted Reba. 'We're almost Earthside,' he said.

'Yes, I know. Starson told me. We're taking a transitube to Underdenver. I'll need clothes before appearing at Central Census in the morning.'

'Underdenver? That's a rather risky excursion, isn't it?'

'It would be without Tourtabs. Starson has forged several that will let us spend the night there safely. We'll be going as legitimate citizens. The Tourtabs will place us off-limits to the Illegals.'

'Why Underdenver? Why not Upperdenver?'

Reba made a face. 'It's so dull up there. And colourless. Starson and I have always craved excitement. Underdenver and the Illegals provide it. Why else do you think they issue Tourtabs? The sober citizens of the Uppercities demanded the right to visit the Undercities. Ever since they forcibly segregated the Illegals from the Legals, Tourtripping has been big business.'

'Enjoy yourselves.'

'I came to ask you to come with us. You're not staying shipside, are you?'

'Did Starson send you to ask me?'

'Starson wants you to come. So do I.'

Shannon glanced at the monitor set in the surface of his desk. 'We'll be Earthside in twenty minutes. I'll meet you at the lock.'

The Transitube sped along its single track through the ravines of Upperdenver and at last slowed to a halt outside the metal shaft labelled 'Descent Sector'.

Starson stood up and hurried down the narrow aisle to the exit. Shannon followed Reba, who was already hurrying after Starson. The three of them stepped into the tubular shaft and held on to the rungs set in its surface. The door circled shut behind them, and they felt the slight giddiness that signalled descent. It quickly passed, and for the next few minutes they had no sensation of movement.

The tube eased to a halt and a small square section at eye level in its surface became transparent. From the audiation system came the recorded request to display Tourtabs. They held up their forged Tabs and were promptly processed. The tube continued its downward descent. When the door at last slide aside a few minutes later, they stepped out of the sterilising enclosure, where a faint hissing was the only sign that they were being vaporised against the diseases that stalked the streets and homiciles of Underdenver. The hissing soon stopped, and a metallic voice crackled, 'Your Tourtabs are validated for nine hours. You will report back here for surfacing at ten o'clock. Failure to report will result in the necessity to search for you and therefore forfeiture of Tourtab privileges for six months. Your guide waits without. Northstates Crimenet offers this warning, "There but for the grace of Crimenet go you." '

They stepped out of the sterilising chamber and found their guide waiting for them. He was a tall man with shoulders like barrels and hands like pumpkins. He took their Tourtabs, glanced at them, and then handed them back. 'We have a number of attractions in Underdenver,' he said, beginning his familiar spiel. 'Perhaps the lady would like to see the Casinos? You gentlemen might prefer the Lottery. Then there are the Matches and, of course, the Games.' His voice lowered, and his nostrils dilated. There are a number of other places of interest that are not normally part of the tour, but a visit to them could be arranged if your interest is strong enough.'

'Come with us for a few blocks,' Shannon said. 'Then disappear. We don't want a guide.'

The guide took the Tokens Shannon thrust at him and dropped them in his pocket. 'Follow me, please.'

As soon as they stepped away from the platform, they were surrounded by children who screamed their wares and hopped about them in eager agitation but did not touch them. Touching Tourtrippers was strictly forbidden. Tourtrippers were protected in the Undercities by their Tourtab status from any touch or other potential danger. The system had worked for nearly fifty years. When it was discovered that what had been for so long euphemistically called 'organised crime' could not be wiped out despite the platitudes of politicians and the occasional crackdown on graft in Crimenet and in Corporations Consolidated, crime was instead segregated. The Undercities were born. Two worlds; two systems. There was, of course, interaction between them, which was deemed 'necessary'. Crime was contained in the Undercities so that citizens of the Uppercities need no longer

89

fear its manifestations. Although the Undercity criminals still served both societies — in secret — it was in a way that left the streets safe in the Uppercities, and only commercial paper bore testament to the interwoven fabric of the two societies.

'The ones wearing red,' Starson commented, pointing to several of the children, 'belong to the assassin caste. Note the daggers they wear in their belts. Those are bullets strung on the necklaces of the little girls.'

'Those nude ones over there,' Reba said, 'must be — '

'They are,' Starson said. 'Prostitutes. Children of, by, and for the flesh. And look! Those in the ebony jerkins and boots sell the service of blackmail.'

'Come on,' Shannon said impatiently. 'Let's get the little bastards out of the way.' He turned to the guide. More Tokens changed hands, with the result that Shannon now held the guide's electronic eel in his hand. He raised it high above his head and brought it sparking down among the children, who screamed at its painful touch and went scurrying out of sight in search of more receptive Tourtrippers.

'We don't need you anymore,' Shannon told the guide.

The guide left.

'Where to?' Starson asked.

'First, my clothes,' Reba said.

'Hey!' Starson yelped. 'I know a place on Hangtree Square that specialises in Uppercity fantasy. That's the place for you, Reba! Let's go there!'

Shannon followed them. They were several paces ahead of him, striding along, hand in hand, like two happy children in a suddenly found playground. He could hear them chattering together. He had difficulty believing that these young voices belonged to the two people he thought he knew. He had never heard either of them sound so free.

They walked beneath the elevated ramps made of plastoid on which men and women in various stages of undress paraded. They looked up and were amused at the sight of the gilded genitalia and the navels set with winking jewels.

'Bodies to buy!' cried out a gnarled old woman sitting on

the lowest of the ramps, her skinny legs dangling as she sucked on a sweetmeat in the form of a miniature sugared skull. 'Rent a pair! Matching colours. Or mix and match. Man 'r woman! Satisfaction guaranteed. You down there, you Tourtrippers. Give old Granny a break. She hasn't sold a single pound of flesh pudding in a week!'

Starson tossed a Token up to her. She pulled her dangling legs up and scrambled to her feet. She deftly caught the Token as it spun up to her. 'Granny gives good bargains. Just take your pick, handsome. How about his one? Or this?'

'None, Granny,' Starson called up to her. 'I would have picked you, old dear, but the years have cheated you in their passing.'

'May the Devil himself be your darling, then, handsome,' crowed the old woman. 'Why don't you tumble that pretty one beside you? Give her a good thrusting for old Granny!'

Reba laughed happily. The old woman grinned down upon them as she went on sucking her sugared skull. Juice slid down her chin from the sweetmeat as the bored bodies about her postured and posed, moved on, and never looked down.

When they arrived at Hangtree Square, they found the Beautyspot in the middle of the block. A huge sculptured figure of a woman reclined, forming the building's façade. Giant plaster feet splayed out on the sidewalk. Far above them were the bent knees. Through the door between the sculptured legs, they went, and found themselves in a purple-and-gold salon heavy with the scent of a mild aphrodisiac.

A young man, ageless, and smooth of face and limb, came towards them. He wore only a satin codpiece and polish on his toenails that caught the light and glinted golden. 'May we serve you all? Or is it to be just you two gentlemen? The lady?'

'She wants clothes,' Shannon replied.

'Monstrous!' exclaimed the young man, puckering his lips and holding his face between his distraught hands as he gazed at Reba's grey coveralls in evident dismay. 'Off! At once! Take them off!'

Reba, thoroughly amused, zipped open her coveralls and stepped out of them.

'Ah!' the young man sighed. 'Now, if you'll just sign this waiver, which will allow the staff to touch you, we'll set you right in a moment or two!' He handed Reba a paper, and she signed it.

'Now, let me see.' He cupped his chin in his hand. 'Fireworms, I think. Yes. And a Sirian scent. Oh, dear, you are such a total challenge! You're so perfectly lovely to begin with! It's really hardly fair!' He lapsed into a pout.

'I'll be back shortly,' Reba said to the two men at her side.

'Fireworms?' Starson whispered in her ear, a mock frown on his face.

'They just might be charming. You mustn't be so provincial.' She laughed aloud, and he seized her hand and swooped to kiss it. She danced away from him and after the young man, who began shooing her into the rear room that was half-hidden from sight by a shimmering curtain of sentient Andromedan crystals that were chiming polyphonically.

CHAPTER ELEVEN

'Starson,' Shannon said, as they waited for Reba to return, 'we'll attack Outerupperdenver while we're here.'

'You've got another contract?'

'Yes. With the Epicureanites in Garth's Galaxy.'

Starson frowned. 'Their tastes, I'm told, are odd. "Bizarre" would probably be a better word.'

'That may be so, but —'

'You know damned well it's so.'

'This time we have certain specifications to meet, so we'll use the cloning technique instead of random selection of fertilised eggs like last time. You and the rest of the crew will locate suitable subjects, and Rawley will do the cell surgery. We'll need one hundred.'

'What are these specifications you refer to?'

'Relatively simple. Fat people. Men or women, it doesn't matter to the Epicureanites. We shouldn't have too much trouble, since Outerupperdenver has an Epicureanite Branch Hostel.'

'You'd sell them their own members?'

'They won't know or care where the clones came from. And in the event that they should find out, they'll be in no position to complain to the authorities. Not when you consider the use to which they intend to put the clones.'

Starson went to the whispering curtain of Andromedan crystals. He touched it, and the melodious murmuring grew louder. He said, 'There's nothing you wouldn't do, is there, Shannon?'

Shannon looked up at him in very real surprise. 'No, nothing.'

Starson shook his head slowly from side to side as he turned and stared at Shannon, trying to decipher the nature of the mechanism that was the man.

'Something wrong, Starson?'

'No, I guess not. It's just that your plan comes as a surprise to me.'

'You'd better sit down before you fall down under the weight of all those scruples you're carrying around with you like excess baggage.'

'Let me tell you something, Starson. Long ago I decided to dispense with the concepts of right and wrong. They can confuse a man, slow him down, even immobilise him. I believe that what works is what's right, and what doesn't is wrong. That's my utilitarian philosophy for getting on in life.'

'I said once before, Shannon, that you were a simple man.'

'And I agreed with you. Starson, come *on*! Think about it. Man, use your head! The Epicureanites want clones that will develop into fat babies. Where would you be liable to find hosts from which you could clone with some guarantee that the developing individuals would be fat?'

'The Epicureanites themselves.'

'Precisely. So . . .'

'So we'll raid the Epicureanite Branch Hostel and . . . all's well that ends well.'

Starson fell silent.

Shannon closed his eyes and then quickly opened them as he heard something silken stirring nearby. A black panther was padding towards him. He remained motionless. The panther stopped six inches from his outthrust legs.

'Come, Caligula,' said the woman who appeared in the outer doorway. She repeated the name a second time, and the panther's lips parted, and a low growl, more of a moan, issued from its throat. It backed away from Shannon, its muscles rippling beneath its pelt, the fire in its eyes roaring.

The woman passed through the crystalline curtain. The panther followed her, pawing at the lowest of the crystals.

'What the hell is keeping Reba?' Starson complained.

Starson, Shannon thought. Another panther. Sleek, and in his way, as deadly as the one that had just vanished. 'A woman dressing is like the building of Rome, Starson. She cannot be hurried, and she must not be cheated of her growing glory. Like Rome, she will emerge when the time is right and all the omens salubrious.'

Starson laughed. 'I'd prefer it, I think, if a woman dressing were more like Old Faithful. Predictable and dependable.'

'You'd give up the pleasure of anticipation? A mistake, I assure you.'

They sat and continued to wait for most of another hour as customers came and went, glancing now and then in their direction with speculative eyes and calculating expressions on their faces. Were they potential customers for death, for odd desires, or perhaps the fruits of certain technological witcheries unavailable to the subdued citizens of the Uppercities? Would they want to touch the heart of an ion activator which was said to provide a thrill akin to a Blavatskian migration of the soul? But Shannon and Starson gave no indication of interest, and only the slightest show of curiosity. The customers came and went. The crystals sang their sibilant song.

The woman with the panther came back through the curtain. She was no longer pink and rosy. Where her skin had been, there now lay a sleek artifical pelt that matched that of the panther's. The panther's ears had been set with gleaming simstones.

Reba came through the curtain a few minutes later. Shannon almost sprang from his chair at the sight of her, but managed to restrain himself. The only sign he gave of being impressed with her remarkable appearance was the way his body seemed to quiver, resisting the ministrations of the chair in which he sat.

'Fireworms!' Reba declared, raising her right hand.

Tiny flashes of light swarmed around her hand, winking like multicoloured jewels. She raised her other hand, and more jewels blazed. 'Look.' She held up the first finger of each of her hands and wiggled them with obvious pleasure. 'Two of their queens are trapped inside these rings. See how they all swarm when I move my fingers!'

She was wearing a necklace that lay low on her throat. From it, light waves of varying spectral intensities cascaded. They blended to produce new tints and combinations of hues. Occasionally they revealed the nakedness of her body beneath them, which had been dusted with yellow petitpaint and touched at strategic locations with droplets of condensed Sirian scent. Her hair was arranged high on her head, a lustrous nest for the sun of itself.

She was an avalanche of sensuality. The Sirian scent, faintly aphrodisiacal, provoked. The fireworms sparkling about her hands made her every gesture a jewelled symphony. And the light cascading from the necklace at her throat gave her the appearance of being constantly in motion.

'Two thousand Tokens,' she said.

Shannon was staring at her in undisguised awe and admiration.

Sarson reached into his pocket and handed her the Tokens. She took them, disappeared, and then returned a moment later from beyond the crystal curtain. She was holding out her hands and smiling brightly. 'I'm quite ready now – for anything. Shall we go?'

Shannon got up at once and started for the door.

'Wait!' she cried out to him. 'Come here, Shannon. You too, Starson.'

When they were beside her, she directed them both to bend their heads. They did, and she poured a catalytic agent from a tiny vial upon their hair. At once the strands of hair on their heads separated, came together, and separated again. In their serpentine writhing, they gave off a golden electrical glow that was visible even in the bright light of the room in which they stood. When they raised their heads, Reba pointed to the large mirror on the wall. They gazed into it and saw their reflections.

Reba said, 'You both look like saints with your halos. Which one of you will lead me to the Promised Land?'

Starson, grinning, bowed her to the door. 'Not saints,' he corrected. 'We look, I think, more like archangels. I shall be Michael. And Shannon ... well, you do look a bit like Lucifer. After the Fall.'

They linked arms and went out into the chaos and cacophony that was Underdenver.

Shannon changed places with Starson so that he could walk on the side of Reba that would leave his right arm free to wield the electronic eel. As they strolled up the street, he used it to clear a path for them through the throng of beggars that materialised from nowhere and descended upon them. The beggars whined and wheedled and cajoled and cried. They displayed their wounds and their running sores that were the obvious products of cosmetisurgery and asked for alms. As Shannon whipped them away, the beggars shouted consonantal curses at them.

They turned the corner and confronted a spectacle that

might have been designed for a warped child. A woman, neither young nor old, neither lovely nor ugly, gyrated before them in a sad parody of grace. Around her neck was a thick collar to which was attached a long leather leash. Holding the other end of the leash and jerking it cruelly to stifle the demented woman's shrill and wordless cries was a crouching baboon.

They walked past the scene, and as they did so, Starson dropped a Token in the tin cup the woman was banging on the pavement at his feet. They entered an alcove that led to a brightly lighted restaurant. A man with a bald head and dark scowl met them and escorted them to the banks of aeroautos parked in the lobby. They got in the nearest one, and it lifted under Shannon's guidance and soared up past the aquatic tanks and the cages and the hydroponic compartments from which they would select items for their meal.

Reba chose a young rock python that lay coiled somnolently under the intense artificial light above it. She ordered fermented marsh grass and selected a liqueur from a bubbling vat. Her choices, punched into the panel of the aeroauto, were recorded on the master grid in the restaurant's kitchen.

Shannon selected a large lobster that had been mutated to eliminate its exoskeleton and increase its fleshy mass. He told Reba, 'I don't like the look in its eyestalks, so I'll put it out of its misery.'

Starson announced that he wasn't hungry, and Shannon glanced covertly at him, suddenly remembering the hours Starson was accustomed to spending alone with the mice in the cargo hold.

They took seats in an intimate rotunda, and twenty minutes later their meals were served by silent androids. The python appeared, spiced and sauced, in the form of lean flank steaks. Reba declared, after her first mouthful, that it was indeed delicious.

Shannon ate as much of the lobster as he could manage, but found that it was considerably larger than it had appeared in its tank. More than half of it remained on his plate when he declared himself no longer hungry.

Throughout the meal, Starson drank heavily. He emptied several small bottles of *rouge nuit* and then called for a keg of *sera febbre*. He raised his glass to Reba and said, 'To yesterday.'

She looked at him with a faint trace of apprehension on her features.

'Reba,' he persisted, 'a toast.' He held his glass high. 'A toast to all our ended yesterdays.'

Reba reached for her glass, and the fireworms glittered about her fingers. She touched her glass to Starson's. 'No, to tomorrow.'

'Ah,' he said, 'a woman of probabilities. You would rather dream of tomorrows than regret your yesterdays.' He drank, coughed, and wiped his lips. 'Shannon, how shall we toast you? What was it that you told me before? That what works is what's right, and what fails is what's wrong? Do you hear that, Reba? That philosophy makes me think of corpses lying in the streets. In it, I hear the wailing of love betrayed and—'

Shannon said, 'Shove it, Starson!' His fists had formed bastions on both sides of his plate.

Starson widened his eyes in an expression of mock surprise, raised his glass, and drank again. 'Love betrayed. Now, there is a subject to redden the eyes of sleepless poets, wouldn't you agree, Shannon? Reba, tell this man, this Master of Myth, about love betrayed and of the betrayers. Go on. Tell him. Let the bell of your voice toll in his ears, and never mind the fact that it tolls for all of us.'

Shannon started to rise, but Starson quickly caught his arm. 'So early an end to our lovely evening, Shannon? Why, the fun is only just beginning. We can visit the Casinos, where a man may win or lose his life. There are bound to be suitable games available here in Underdenver for even a player as sophisticated as you.'

Shannon shook his arm free of Starson's grip. He glanced at Reba, saw her nod, hesitated, and then sat down.

Starson held out his keg of *sera febbre* to Shannon, but Shannon covered his glass.

'*Serra febbre*,' Starson murmured. 'Evening fever.' He paused. His next words were breathy, barely audible. 'I burn with it.' He looked across the table at Shannon. 'Fever brings strange dreams. As the Mythmaster, Shannon, what would you suggest I do about these dreams, these solitary myths of mine?'

'Deny them,' Shannon said flatly.

'What? Become Judas? Did you hear that, Reba? He would have me deny my dreams. Ah, so sly, this Mythmaster. As sly and as full of defences as a Space Patrol ship. So be it, then. I deny you, Shannon. I will no longer dream you. And, Reba, I now vanquish you from my dreams as well.'

'You can't,' Reba said.

Her words seemed to irritate Starson. He drew back his lips in the manner of a predator approaching his prey. The emerald in his front tooth flashed. He said, 'Too many others have stolen me, and too many others have defeated you. No, Reba, we are no longer the nearly innocent children we once were.'

'But love does not die,' Reba said quietly. 'It grows old, true, but it increases in value as it does.'

Shannon watched her face and saw the real pain welling in her eyes as she spoke to Starson.

Starson's voice was harsh when he spoke again. 'You talk like a broker speculating in capital markets. "It increases in value." ' He gave a bitter laugh, 'No, Reba. Love merely grows old, and it sickens and becomes pale, and its breath turns foul. It's eyes are clouded, and where once it walked, it limps.' He drank. 'I loved you, Reba. I did. Can you remember our yesterday?'

'Yes.'

'And what about you, Shannon? Tell us of your yesterdays and of the women you loved. Then explain to us why you are all alone today.'

'I am alone because I choose to be alone. I came into the world alone, and all the rest is merely chance encounter. It is easy to be with someone. All a man must do is to lie skillfully and always.'

'Now it is revealed!' Starson crowed, but there was no merriment in his voice. 'Now we see the myths that the Master himself employs to sustain himself.'

'Starson,' Reba said, 'stop wanting what doesn't exist.'

'The day I stop the wanting, I will die. Don't you see that it is the wanting that matters? It isn't the object wanted that is important. As you suggest, what I want may not exist, but that doesn't stop me from wanting it. No, I am not yet ready to die.'

Reba leaned over to Shannon and whispered, 'You could help him. And without really hurting yourself.'

'Let him make love to me? Is that what you mean? You would have me cheat him that way?'

'Lie to him, Shannon. It would be a kindness.'

'He would know it was a lie.'

'Yes,' he would. But Starson has had long practice in pretending. He would willingly believe your lie.' Reba stood up quickly and walked around the table. She put out a hand, and Starson took it, looking up at her in surprise. The fireworms swirled around their linked hands as Reba led him out to the Low-G area, where they danced in a buoyant, nearly weightless state.

When they returned to the table, Shannon did not catch their words, but he did recognise the urgency of Reba's tone. Starson seemed about to raise an objection to whatever it was that she had said, but by then they were at the table.

'Shannon?' Reba stood beside him, waiting.

He rose and followed her into the Low-G area and felt the effects of the reduced gravity at once. He began to feel lighter in mind as well as body as Reba floated above him, and he rose up to her while the music sidled out and surrounded them, and they touched lightly and then embraced, rolling pleasantly, almost giddily, in the air above the floor that seemed so far below.

When the music ended, they returned to the table to find that Starson had ordered another bottle of *rouge nuit* and had filled their glasses.

Shannon was about to protest that he wanted no more

when he felt Reba's hand touch his thigh beneath the table.

'One final toast,' Starson was saying. 'To the wanting.'

They drained their glasses.

Almost immediately, Shannon knew that something was wrong. Reba's face seemed impossibly distant. As he looked across the table at Starson, he felt the room shift as if it were settling in the first shock of a tremor. Starson had done something to his drink. Shannon felt himself becoming Mythmad as Reba stood up and seemed to float away from the table and disappear from sight. He glanced through a rising, shimmering haze at Starson.

'I will not hurt you,' Starson said from miles away. 'I hurt only myself.'

The haze swept down upon Shannon, blurring the angles of the room, muting the music and his own barely audible protests. He knew it was too late to save himself from what was to come. With the advent of Mythmadness, reality withdrew and spectres walked abroad, freed from the locked prisons of his own Mythmad mind. He felt himself surrendering. He was letting go, slipping away from himself. Before Starson reached out to take his hand and lead him from the table, Shannon heard the tinkle of breaking glass. He looked down slowly at the table that was vanishing beneath him and wondered why he had shattered such an innocent object as the glass that now lay in fragments on the floor. He looked up again, wondering why Starson looked so sad.

He felt himself moving through the streets of Underdenver. Was it the dead Devlin who moved so eerily beside him? No, it was another young man with a forlorn face. Who, Shannon asked himself, had robbed that face of joy?

The room in which he found himself, after an eternity of walking, was dark and heavy with the smell of ... Incense? No. The odour of flesh against flesh. The air was alive with musk of lust. The room tilted and swayed, and it was some time before Shannon realized that it was he who reeled and not the room. The young man beside him was coming towards him, and he knew the man, had known him. The grip of the man's hand was strong on his arm, and he looked down at the white knuckles and the many rings. The tiny hairs on the hand became a forest in which he wandered, temporarily lost.

He was being led to the bed. Undressed. He saw Starson reach out to flick the switch that would totally darken the room, and then stop at the sound of a stricken cry. His cry. The cry of the hunter? Or the cry of the prey that begs the moon to throw down its light so that a means of escape might yet be discovered.

Starson left the lights as they were. Shadows moved in the room as he reached out and touched Shannon. Five shadowy rods flickered over Shannon's face and tangled hair. Momentarily distracted, Shannon watched them. And then, with a sigh, Starson bent down to a familiar feasting.

A fury, escaped, stalked the shadows. Shannon found himself engaged in a primal battle. But when he tried to ascertain the nature of his enemy, he found only warm flesh and heard only whispered words that were too tender to have come from the lips of any enemy he had ever known. He felt himself as separate at first from this other, this one unknown, and then, suddenly, a vital part of him. Where did he begin, and where did this other man end — this man who was touching his body with, yes, reverence? Were they one?

He found himself on his feet, and they were indeed one as the shadows wrapped themselves around the odd construction they had become. At his feet, Shannon saw someone kneeling and wondered how he had become a god. He felt the unfamiliar fingers sliding up and down the inner surfaces of his thighs, and he marvelled at the fires that had been lighted within him. And then, in an uncontrollable surge of joy, he bent down and raised the worshipper up, and they were linked, locked together, and the shadows remained, for a time, at bay.

And then they fell, a twinned tower, crumbling. The bed shuddered under their impact, and the words went on. Fragmented, Tortured. Joyless.

Shannon saw the image of the glass he had broken earlier, but this — this body now beneath his own — was not that glass. Was it?

Starson's touch was hot and skilled. Beneath it, Shannon rolled away, out of the world and then back into it, and finally all the Starsons in the world were upon him and in him, and he cried out in pain and pleasure. He felt every drop of sweat that beaded his body as a separate entity, and he forgot completely that his face was scarred and his leg destined forever to limp as it carried him from world to world.

Someone's tears tasted salty suddenly on his tongue. And then, again, there was only the stormy harbour of his thighs in which the ship that was Starson had chosen to anchor. Starson's head bobbed in its tempestuous haven, and Shannon at last exploded and sank down into a dark and lonely sea, no longer linked to anyone, free.

Alone.

Starson, gleaming with sweat, brought astringents with which he anointed Shannon's body. In his hand was an antidote capsule, which he firmly placed between Shannon's lips. Rising, he stared down to watch the mists of Shannon's Mythmadness whirl away.

Shannon opened his mouth to speak. Starson closed his eyes as if he were afraid to hear the words.

'I lied,' Shannon whispered, and the last shadow in the room died triumphant.

Starson moved away. As he backed towards the door, he memorised the body lying on the bed that was slipping rapidly into sleep. That naked body on the bed spoke silently of power and strength and also of weakness and a pain that had nothing to do with scars or injured legs. It told of the pain that a man feels when he is determined to protect himself from love and discovers that he has failed.

'I was a door, Shannon,' Starson said softly. 'You have passed through me and will go on. Tonight I met you for the first time. And tonight you have bade me good-bye, because that is the way it must be for both us.' He picked up his clothes and began to dress, trying not to think, desperately trying not to care.

CHAPTER TWELVE

Shannon was awakened the next morning by a shrill and petulant cry. He sat up in the bed, startled and blinking, and saw the man who was wearing a kimono pointing at him and crying out and waving his hands about in angry agitation.

'Hoist your ass out of there, hustler! You paid till eight a.m., and it's ten past already!' The man's rouged cheeks were lanterns, but there was no matching light in his eyes. He was emaciated, and beneath his wet lips, his teeth were yellow and broken. 'Come on, you two,' he yelled back through the door that was open behind him. To Shannon he said, 'Your lover left this note for you.'

Shannon took it from him and hurriedly began to dress.

A woman came into the room followed by a girl who bore a blue salamander on one scrawny shoulder. The two of them stared at Shannon as he fumbled into his clothes. The girl ambled up to him and put her hand on the belt he was trying to buckle. 'Listen, if you want, you can stay. I do anything. So does she. To anybody.' The girl jerked a thumb over her shoulder at the other woman, who was lighting a scentspray. 'It won't cost you nothing, because we already paid, and it might be fun, you know? You look like you got what it takes. Want to show me?'

Shannon pushed past her as the man in the kimono tore the sheets from the bed and screamed something about an extra charge for stains all over everything. But Shannon was gone.

Outside the decrepit building, he unfolded the note the man had given him and read what Starson had written. He was to meet Starson and Reba at Central Census at nine.

He crumpled the note and tossed it into the gutter. As he watched it soak up the slime there, he thought about the previous night. He couldn't remember clearly what had happened. But he could guess. He remembered the restaurant and Reba's suggestion that he let Starson ... Had he? There had been the drink. The Mythmadness. What, he wondered, had come afterwards? He felt violated. Had he violated Starson, and if so, in what manner? A feeling of anger raged through him momentarily. He was not angry at the ... the contact that had probably taken place. He had done worse, and often. He believed there was nothing wrong with finding sexual satisfaction with a person of one's own gender. Shame was unnecessary. Guilt was archaic. He knew that there were a few of the Space Patrol ships themselves that were manned with pairs of men chosen carefully for the degree of their mutual love in order to help ensure valour in battle. Lovers made the best fighters, the Patrol had discovered in this enlightened age. They fought not only for their own survival but also for that of the beloved.

Then what caused the anger he was feeling? He was angry, he began to realise, because he could not remember what had happened. Starson had cheated him. In his lust, he had undoubtedly indulged himself, and at the same time, wiped Shannon's memory clean. He cursed and strode up the street, heading fo Upperdenver.

Reba and Starson were waiting for him outside the building that housed Central Census.

'It's almost time to say good-bye,' Reba said as he joined them. Her voice was calm. Her fireworms had vanished in the night with the stars. Her hair had been redone in a more sedate fashion, and she was wearing a simple green gown that bared only her ankles.

'You've reregistered?' Shannon inquired.

105

'Not yet. They've just opened. Come in with me. I'd like you both to know my new locus.'

Starson said to Shannon, 'Good morning.'

Shannon ignored him. There was nothing in Starson's expression that revealed his feelings or attitudes. His face was neither triumphant nor disdainful. He looked neither happy nor sad.

They went inside and were directed by the code clerk to the proper cubicle. Reba stood before the Census Set and punched in her identification digits and then spoke into the receptor. She told the machine that she had lost her identity status and current assignment and wanted to reregister.

The machine told her to wait. A moment late, it's electronic voice announced that reregistration was impossible.

'But why?' Reba cried, annoyed.

'Reba Charlo,' the machine replied, 'has been declared without legal sanction and as an Illegal can be given no identification papers for use in any Uppercity.'

'I'll appeal,' Reba protested.

'No appeal possible. This order has been signed by the magistrate of Interworld Tribunal. However, there is a codicil.'

'A codicil?' Reba waited impatiently.

'Reba Charlo may redeem her current status as an Illegal, provided she agree to return to her previous locus and remain there under the probationary aegis of Oxon Kaedler.'

Reba's hands clenched at her sides. She turned swiftly and strode out of the cubicle with Shannon and Starson following her. Behind them, they heard the machine babbling: 'Illegals will be summarily shot upon identification in any Uppercity of Earth, and their remains will be unclaimable by kin and they . . .'

'Kaedler!' Reba exclaimed as they came out of the building.

'He isn't about to let you get away from him,' Starson commented. 'He may be legally dead, but that hasn't stopped him from bribing the magistrate and bending the law.'

106

'Forget Kaedler,' Shannon said. 'Starson can forge new identity papers for you. How long will it take, Starson?'

Starson shrugged. 'A day or two. Three at the most.'

'You can stay with us for that length of time, Reba,' Shannon said, 'Or if you prefer, you can go down to one of the Undercities.'

'No more than three days, Starson?' Reba asked.

He nodded.

Reba, as she weighted her options, bit her lower lip.

'Let's head back to the ship,' Shannon suggested.

Reba hesitated and then said, 'Wait. I want to try something. It will take only a minute.' She walked down the street and went into a shop.

Shannon and Starson entered behind her and heard her ask the clerk behind the counter for a supply of scentsprays. She told him that she had lost her cashcard but gave him her name and asked him to check Central Census for verification of both her identity and credit status. When the clerk returned after doing so, there was fear on his face. He declared that he didn't dare serve Illegals or he'd be put out of business. Reba asked him what the trouble was. He explained that Central Census had listed her as an Illegal and that she would remain so until she reestablished herself in her previous locus.

Outside the shop, Reba said to Starson, 'You can forget about the forged identity papers. Kaedler's fixed it so that I can't do anything or go anywhere, even legally. You'd have to put my picture on the papers. Even if I used a different name, I'd still be recognised by the optical scanners.'

'We can talk about it back on the ship,' Shannon said. 'Come on.'

They walked in silence to the Transitube Terminal and boarded a car that carried them soundlessly to their destination. They walked the remaining distance to the ship. Throughout their brief journey, Shannon had found himself occasionally touching Reba, as if to guide her or protect her. His hand now and then found her elbow. He placed his arm around her waist at one point and another time he clasped her hand in his. He suspected the reason for his gestures. He was making a declaration to himself and to Starson that would deny the reality of the previous night. *See*, said his flesh against Reba's, *I am a man and this is a woman and thus it shall be for me. What happened last night was of no importance. I know the nature of my desires.*

Shannon, when he reached the command cabin of the ship, ordered Starson to plot course for the imminent raid on Outer-upperdenver. It would occur at noon, he decided. As he was about to leave, Starson said, 'Last night is over, Shannon. In a way, I'm sorry it happened. In a way, I'm not.'

Shannon's eyes narrowed and stiffened. 'Mythmadness brings counterfeit dreams. You know that. No alchemy ever known can turn the lead of lust into the gold of love.' He had not known what the words would be when they finally came, as they had just now done, but he had known that they would have to be harsh and that they would have to hurt. The expression on Starson's face told him that they had fulfilled their purpose.

'Mythmadness,' Starson said. 'is its own reality. It feeds on the victim's own madnesses. Madness is merely a symptom of the failure of reality contact. But madmen were at certain times and in certain places thought to be divine.'

'I don't love you,' Shannon said. 'I never could.'

Starson seemed not to have heard the remarks. He went on speaking, his eyes focused on a point just to the right of where Shannon was standing so stiffly. 'They called those madmen "touched". They had been "touched" by the finger of some god. They were revered and envied as well as feared. I cherish my own madness, Shannon, if that is what you would call it. Some tricky god has touched me, and now I walk on no main highway.'

'Should you ever try again to ...' Shannon left the sentence unfinished. There was a need, he felt, to complete the slaughter. He had to make sure of something not quite fully comprehended. 'In the future, you might consider proper payment instead of resorting to Mythmadness. Enough Tokens might make me ... amenable.'

Starson shuddered visibly. Shannon's knife had tasted the throat of the sacrificial animal, and blood was everywhere.

'I have already paid,' Starson said. 'Last night, I paid.'

'I don't mean for that filthy room.'

'Neither do I. I mean that I paid in a currency that is not calculable in your terms.'

Shannon muttered an obscenity.

Starson did not flinch from it. He almost seemed to welcome it in the sense that a sufferer under the cruel hands of the torturer may begin to believe in his own guilt. 'Do you remember anything about last night, Shannon?'

'It was not I who was with you last night. It was some Mythmad man.'

'Anything you said?'

'It was not me who spoke. It was the Mythmadness.'

'Yes. The Mythmadness. Perhaps it was only that.'

Shannon left the command cabin and the battle he had waged there, unsure of whether he was victor or vanquished, certain only of the fact that it had been a dangerous duel.

He met Lee Rawley in the corridor. Rawley grabbed his arm as he strode past.

'Hey, Shannon! Give a greeting, man! Don't go careening by like some damned orbitless derelict!'

'Sorry, Rawley. I was thinking.'

'Deep thoughts, no doubt, to make your old friends and colleagues in crime invisible. How was your visit to Underdenver?'

'Don't leer. It was . . . Underdenved. Enough said.'

'I hear you have another strike lined up.'

'Yes. Before leaving here, we'll hit Outerupperdenver. The Epicureanite Branch Hostel there. We'll use the cloning technique this time. A total of one hundred individual cells are called for in the contract.' Shannon explained the nature of the contract, and Rawley whistled through his teeth. 'Check with Starson. He's in the command cabin. He'll give you the co-ordinates and the timing. I've briefed him. He's alerting the crew.'

Shannon left Rawley and headed for the cabin Reba occupied. When he stood before it, he knocked loudly. When there was no immediate response, he pounded his fist on the door and then opened it.

'I was bathing,' Reba said, stepping out of the sanicube. She belted a crewman's robe about herself and sat down. 'You look like a clam that someone has stepped on.'

'Are you planning on staying shipside, or are you going Undercity?'

She hesitated, examining Shannon's face. Something seemed definitely wrong. He was looking at the robe that bulked about her body, leaving only her lower legs bare. 'Does it matter? Would you want me aboard? After all, I'm evidently Kaedler's prey, and he's a determined hunter, as we've already seen. I would be a liability shipside.'

'We're going to hit Outerupperdenver in less than an hour. It's a dangerous mission, as always. You might be better off in some Undercity.'

'I'll stay aboard, if it's all right with you.'

Shannon sat down. So it had happened. He had wanted to hear her say those words, and now she had said them. He felt curiously disappointed.

'Can you risk carrying such a dangerous cargo?'

He got up and went to her. He lifted her to her feet and eased her robe over one shoulder.

'This is not Seventh Heaven,' she said.

'Shipside, you're another crew member in my employ.' Why did the words come out so wrong? Once he had known how to be tender. Why now did he sound so autocratic? Desperately, he bent and pressed his lips to her exposed breast.

Reba looked down at his bent head. 'If we agree that I am to remain shipside, then certain matters must be understood by both of us.'

He raised his head and stared at her stonily.

'If I want you and if you want to be wanted that way, we will come together. We are two rational and independent human beings. However, if employment by you means rendering sexual services, then I will leave.'

Shannon seized her arms, and as he did so, her robe opened. 'I want you,' he muttered. 'Now.'

'You need me, Shannon. That is something quite different.'

'Yes, it's true. I need you.'

Reba shook her head. 'You need me now to prove that you needn't fear Starson. Was it so awful last night?'

He wanted to shout to drown out her words. He wanted to strike her. He wanted to do something to establish things as he knew they should be. 'Reba,' he muttered. 'You know I . . .'

'I know you are afraid.'

'Starson doesn't frighten me!'

'Your feelings about him do.'

'Of all the women I have tumbled, Reba, of all the women I have hoisted, you are . . .' He buried his face between her breasts and felt her heart beating.

She said nothing for a long moment. And then, with a sigh, she loosened her robe and let it fall from her. She led Shannon to the bunk bolted to the wall and brought him down upon her. She spread her legs as he fumbled with his clothes, and then expertly fitted herself to him. She said nothing as he lunged and thrust himself into her, clutching her shoulders so hard that they hurt.

He tried to drown himself in her. He rocked savagely above and within her, but despite the skill with which she received him, he knew that Reba Charlo was filled with pity for him. Her eyes, when he caught fleeing glimpses of them in his urgency, were sorrowful, and he suddenly knew himself to be one large, raw wound to which she ministered with kindness and a degree of despair that matched his own.

As the ship approached the sprawling suburbopolis that was Outerupperdenver, Shannon sent out a distress call that would lure the Patrol to a nonexistent spacer and thus keep them away from his own ship during the impending raid.

When they were a mile above Outerupperdenver and circling, he gave the order to release the pellets on the chosen target. He boarded the single pod that would be used during the raid. Starson and Rawley joined him a moment later.

They waited only long enough for the pellets to induce Mythmadness before launching the pod from its anchorage in the belly of the ship. It soared downwards, unfolding the long spindles of its legs, and landed on the enteramp leading to the central mall of the Epicureanite Branch Hostel.

Shannon leaped from the pod, followed by Starson and Rawley. He flung open the hostel doors, and Starson bounded through them with his glowgas gun freed of its holster.

Ringing the huge mall were voluptuous statues of men and women engaged in sensual revels. A gigantic cornucopia dominated the area from which flowed, in steady and haphazard profusion, platters heaped high with succulent roasts and fleshy fruits and an occasional live animal trussed and ready for the infrared ovens.

Sprawled on brocaded couches, lying drooling and dazed on dais and low caravan, were the residents of the hostel. Garlands of flesh ringed their necks and drooped to their chests. Eyes like nuts in the puddings of faces glared or stared wildly at the invaders, while some of the people cried out and tried to rise but were toppled by the combination of their own gargantuan proportions and the giddying effects of the Mythmadness in which they wallowed. There were screams and moans that fluttered up to nest in the tangled limbs of the statuary overhead.

Starson moved lithely among the Mythmad, marking a man here, a woman there, with a purple blast from his glowgas gun. Rawley, following in his wake, bent to those identified, and using a surgical needle, deftly plucked cells from earlobes and fingers and chins, after which he sprayed a freezing antiseptic on the minuscule wounds and moved on, playing his role in the swift ballet being performed by himself, Starson, and Shannon.

While the cells were being stolen, Shannon acted as shepherd. When those of the Epicureanites who could manage to move wandered too close to doors or windows, he shoved and kicked them back into the centre of the mall and into Starson's path. He reached up and fouled the alarm system. 'One hundred,' he called out to remind Rawley. 'Take a few extra in case there's damage to some of them.'

Rawley signalled that he had heard, and went on bending and rising and moving on, the vials in his belt swinging slightly with his movements, tinkling gaily against one another, the only music accompanying his grotesque gavotte.

Shannon examined the gilded cornucopia. Beneath its gaudiness, he saw that it contained a simple conveyor belt that wound up and out of sight to some source of food at its tip which was hidden beneath drapes of a gauzy material hanging from the ceiling.

They moved into other rooms, where men and women roiled and writhed nakedly together, all temporarily demented. The forms that their Mythmadness took were both picturesque and picaresque. They slobbered their visions of gluttony. They barked their desires and fumbled about, fondling themselves and one another.

'How many, Rawley?' Shannon called out.

'Fifty-four,' came the answer.

'That's all of them,' Starson called out from an anteroom. 'Unless you want some of the thinner ones.'

'No,' Shannon yelled back. 'Make up the difference with duplicate cells.' He indicated the first group of Epicureanites whom Starson had marked. 'Hurry it up!'

Ten minutes later, Rawley announced that he had one hundred and nine cells.

Shannon headed back towards the mall. He passed the cornucopia, which was still mindlessly spilling out food and splaying it out over the already full tables. He lifted a flagon containing an orange liquid and drank from it. He set it down, wiped his lips, and happily patted the plaster posterior of a wood nymph who was being willingly penetrated by a winged griffin.

They ran down the enteramp and climbed aboard the pod. Within seconds they were airborne, and soon afterwards had docked in the belly of the ship. Starson went at once to the command cabin to plot their course for Garth's Galaxy, and Rawley headed for his laboratory, where he would freeze the pirated cells for the duration of the flight.

Shannon was about to enter his cabin when Reba appeared in the corridor. 'I watched your foray on the screen. It seemed to go well.'

'Yes, it did.'

'What will be done with those cells you stole?'

'The Epicureanites will mature them. Are you familiar with the process?'

'No,' Reba said, following him into his cabin. 'I'm no scientist.'

'It's a matter clonal reproduction,' he told her. 'These cells will have their nuclei removed by the Epicureanites, which will then be implanted in human female egg cells in which the nucleus has been destroyed. After that, they'll be subjected to growth stimulation and acceleration in the artificial wombs, and the results will be perfect replicas of the original cell donors.'

'Why did you choose only the fattest of the Epicureanites as donors?'

'The Epicureanites, as you may know, have rather strange and somewhat experimental tastes.'

'I don't understand.'

'They plan to use the replicas for food.' Shannon stepped into the sanicube and turned on the spray. When he came out sometime later, Reba stared coldly at him.

'You don't care,' she said.

He belted his trousers and bent to buckle his boots. 'Care? About what?'

'About what's going to happen to the people that will be grown from those cells.'

'No, frankly, I don't. I will deliver the cells as my contract call for. Beyond that the matter is of no concern to me.'

'But it has to be! Reba protested. 'It just has to be! You're an accessory before the fact of murder!'

Shannon sat down across from her. 'My only crime is theft. If murder is to be committed —'

'You said it would be.'

'All right. When the murders are committed, it will have nothing at all to do with me. I won't be the one who prepares the ovens. I will be neither chef nor diner.'

'Doesn't anything sicken you? Couldn't you have gotten cells from cattle — from anything except human beings?'

'The contract specifically calls for human cells,' Shannon answered calmly.

Reba stood up and began to pace the room. She avoided looking at Shannon lounging in his chair near the door. 'It's obscene. You're obscene! Why, it's unthinkable, and yet you've done it and seem satisfied.'

'Not yet. I'll be satisfied only when I've been paid.'

Reba turned on him in a fury. 'You once tried to save those prisoners in the solitary cells. How can you participate in murder now?'

Shannon sighed with false distress. 'You still don't — or won't — understand. I will not have participated in murder. The Epicureanites will be the murderers. I am not responsible for their actions.'

'Then your conscience is clear?'

'No, dead. I killed it years ago. So in a way you're right. I am a murderer.' He leaned back in his chair and stretched. 'The cook could use your help in the galley.'

When Reba had gone, after slamming the door behind her, Shannon frowned. When whores begin to talk of conscience, he thought, it is time to temper the force of changing winds. Reba obviously had set limits to her life. She would not commit murder. That was one limit. Were there others? It was an interesting speculation. He had thought she was invulnerable. She certainly seemed to be, judging by her generally cool exterior, which was heated only during the sometimes simulated excesses of her profession. And yet she still seemed to be deeply and sincerely involved with Starson. She showed a deep and tender concern for him. If Shannon knew any one thing, it was that no man or woman is invulnerable who can show concern for another human being. So there were indeed definite limits to Reba Charlo's life and her invulnerability. He had not forgotten his first meeting with her, when she had managed to humiliate him by making him feel like an aroused hound with his nose hung high in the air to track the scent of flesh. He began to wonder how she might be brought down, if at all; how she might be stripped of her ability to pity him, as she had done only that morning while he raged within her. Was there a way to violate her conscience? And if there was, and if he could succeed in violating it, what would happen to the proud Reba, so secure in her indignation and her pity that was, in a twisted way, little more than contempt for him? The thought intrigued him as he finished dressing and headed for the command cabin to check the progress of the flight.

CHAPTER THIRTEEN

They were nearly a week out from Earth and almost a day into Garth's Galaxy when Rawley brought the news to Shannon, who was in the exercise room.

'Every goddamned one of them!' Rawley roared, looking as if he were about to explode.

'When?' Shannon snapped.

'Just now. Not ten minutes ago.' Rawley seized two rings embedded in the wall and pulled furiously on them. The muscles in his arms thickened. 'I was in the lab listening to a tapetext. She came in. She said she wanted to talk. She looked stunning, even in those lousy coveralls, with all that hair flowing gloriously around her face and those small hands and —'

'Never mind that.'

'Well, she sat down, and I turned off the tapetext. She asked me about my work, about why I was here — all sorts of things. I hadn't realised how much I needed to talk to someone.' He released the rings and began to pace the floor, shaking his head. 'Well, I told her what she wanted to know, because she really did seem interested. To tell the truth, I was flattered. An ugly old man like me doesn't usually get attention from a woman like Reba Charlo.'

'Go on.'

'She wanted coffee. Actually, I was the one who suggested we have some. So I left the lab and went down to the galley to get it. When I came back, she was gone.'

'And the cells had been destroyed.'

'Every last one of them. She had raised the temp control high enough to kill them all.'

'Where is she now?'

'How the hell should I know? The point is, what are we going to do?'

Shannon was silent. He stared thoughtfully at the wall and then at Rawley. 'It's too late to turn back. And without cells, we will have wasted the trip and our time. There'll be no pay if there's no delivery. But I intend to make the delivery as planned, if not exactly in accord with the terms of our contract.'

'How —'

Interrupting, Shannon said, 'I intend to deliver cells. Mine — and Reba's. If anyone else aboard wants to volunteer a donation, fine.'

'Not me,' Rawley said quickly and emphatically. 'The thought of what's going to happen to the dupes — no, not me.'

'Get your instruments. I'll meet you at Reba's cabin.'

Rawley, muttering to himself, left the exercise room.

When Shannon reached Reba's cabin, he entered without knocking and found her sitting with her back to the door, calmly listening to a tapetext. Without turning, she said, 'Shannon?'

'Yes.'

'I've been expecting you.'

He positioned himself in front of her, but she refused to meet his eyes. He angrily switched off the tapetext, nearly breaking the control mechanism as he did so. 'Did you think you could void my contract by what you did?' When she didn't answer, he said, 'Well, you failed. I intend to make the delivery as scheduled.'

She looked up at him. 'Impossible. I destroyed every single cell.'

'But you didn't destroy yourself.'

It was obvious that she did not understand his meaning. She continued to stare at him, puzzled. And then her eyes widened slightly, and her lips parted.

'Yes,' he said. 'Your cells will be substituted for some of those you destroyed. Most of the crew, I expect, will donate some. I shall submit some also.

'After Rawley removes the cells from your body, you'll be confined to this cabin for the remainder of the trip. Furthermore, I intend to leave you with the Epicureanites. Misguided moralists aboard a ship like mine are a menace. You can continue your missionary work among the Epicureanites while the cells are being matured.'

'You should have accepted Kaedler's offer,' Reba said. 'You two would have made a good team. Both of you are utterly ruthless men. Shannon, I did what I did for your sake.'

'You did it because you are a fool, Reba. Only fools believe that they have the right to interfere with another person's life. Your experience with Starson should have taught you that.'

'My experience with Starson taught me love. It was the only time in my life when I felt safe and sure of myself with another human being. Oh, you needn't sneer. I suppose I can understand your surprise. You're wondering what Starson can know about love. Well, I tell you that he is a man who knows more about love than most people aboard this ship, and I regretfully include myself in that category. But Starson loved me in a way that ... I'm not sure how to put it. In a way that enriched me because he was so open and so free. He freed me. People do strange things for love.'

'They do them also for hate. As you did.'

Reba shook her head slowly. 'Shannon, you have never learned to tell the difference. You think I destroyed those cells to hurt you in some way. Well, you're wrong. I did it to help the executive officer of the Spacelane Five Fleet who cared more about the impending death of Patrol prisoners than he did about his own future career or safety.'

'Then you did it for a dead man.'

'I hope that's not true. I believe it isn't.'

At that moment, Rawley appeared in the doorway.

'Get busy,' Shannon ordered, with a nod in Reba's direction.

Looking years older than he had at their earlier meeting in the exercise room, Rawley moved slowly towards Reba.

She looked up at him and said, 'Not you, Lee. Shannon must do it.'

Rawley hesitated. Shannon barked an order, and Rawley removed a micropipette from its sterile container. His eyes pleaded with Reba.

'I'll fight you, Lee,' Reba told him.

'Shannon?' Rawley gave him a look of defeat and held out the pipette.

Shannon swore and took it from him.

Reba held out her arms. 'I'm ready, Shannon.'

He took her arm and pushed up the sleeve of her coveralls. He touched the pipette to her skin, and she flinched. 'How the hell do you do it?' he shouted to Rawley. 'I'm no biologist.'

Rawley showed him how to hold the pipette and how to remove and then release the cell into the vial of nutrient solution he was holding.

Shannon tried again, and a red seed of blood appeared on Reba's wrist. 'The damned thing is clogged or something!' he raged. 'Rawley, I order you to —'

'It's all right now, Lee,' Reba said.

'You heard her,' Shannon said, handing the pipette to Rawley.

Starson appeared in the doorway. 'Every member of the crew, myself included, has volunteered to supply cells, Shannon.'

'You told the crew?' Shannon asked Rawley.

'I did.'

'Because we all want our pay,' Starson said. 'There are nineteen of us. Rawley makes twenty.'

'Not me,' Rawley said quickly.

'Then you will make the twentieth donor, Shannon,' Starson said. 'That will mean five cells apiece from each of us. You don't need Reba. You're already cheating in terms of the contract. None of us is fat. So why use Reba?'

Shannon studied Starson's face. There was a faint trace of mockery on his curved lips. But there was something else in his eyes. Accusation. Rawley was watching him too. There was nothing he could do under the circumstances. Starson had won. He began to feel like a fox among too many hunting hounds. But he would give no indication of his unease. The game was being played on a seemingly superficial level. A game of facts, as Starson had defined it. Twenty crew members. Five cells apiece. No, there was nothing he could do. 'Rawley,' he said, 'make the rounds among the crew.'

After Rawley had departed, Starson said to Reba, 'The cook asked if you would help him in the galley.'

'Tell the cook,' Shannon said, 'that Reba will be confined to her cabin for the duration of the trip.'

Starson, surprised at the announcement, mockingly inquired, 'Why not turn her over to the Space Patrol while you're at it.'

'Take care!' Shannon muttered.

'He's going to leave me with the Epicureanites,' Reba told Starson.

'Why, Shannon?' Starson asked in a low tone.'

'I told you before that as commander of this ship I owe no explanations to anyone.'

'Is Reba so deadly?' Are you so vulnerable before her?'

'Yes,' Reba answered, puncturing Shannon's angry silence. 'To both questions — yes. He knows . . . that I love him. I am

120

therefore, to his way of thinking, deadly. And he is therefore vulnerable.'

'So you must be locked up,' Starson commented. 'And later cast away.' He sighed. 'I'll stay with you. We can get to Earth — or somewhere else — aboard one of the supply ships.'

'No, Starson,' Reba protested.

'But it's necessary that I leave too, don't you see? Because I would have to be locked up eventually. For the same reason.'

The battle, Shannon realized, was far from over. Starson was goading him. Or was he speaking the simple truth? 'You will make the return trip to Earth aboard this ship, Starson,' Shannon said. 'We need an astrogator.'

'Several members of the crew, although uncertified, are reasonably well-qualified to astrogate. You've never been particularly concerned about whether or not your crewmen had Patrol certification. No, Shannon, I'll stay with Reba.'

'You will not,' Shannon said flatly.

'Shannon,' Reba said, 'there will never be enough prisons for you.'

'There is really only one,' Starson commented sadly. 'His own. The one in which he has imprisoned himself in order to lock out the world. The one of his skin. The one from which he fires the shots that kill good men like Maxevitch.'

'Get out!' Shannon bellowed. 'Now!'

When Starson had gone, Shannon left the cabin and locked the door behind him. He went to his own cabin and tried to concentrate on the trip records and the crew position reports but failed. He sat back in his chair, his hands gripping the edges of his desk, and let himself surrender to the torrents of anger that flooded through him. Starson was the target of his rage. So was Reba. Starson still believed that he had been the cause of Maxevitch's death. Starson, of course, knew nothing of the order he had issued — the false order — concerning power reduction, which had had the effect of eliminating the auditory stimulation of tapetexts and thus had appreciably reduced Maxevitch's sensory agony during his withdrawal ordeal. All he had to do, Shannon knew, was tell the chief engineer to tell Starson the truth — that there had been no power reduction – and Starson would be able to guess the reason for the order. But no. No, let Starson believe what he wanted to believe. Actually, Shannon thought, Starson believes himself to be another Maxevitch — and my victim. Well, it may be true. Perhaps he is. But no man is another's victim unless he really wants to be.

And what about Reba? He wished now that he had never told her about the solitary cells and his own tarnished history following that incident. By telling her, he had given her power over him. No man should tell a woman about the hurts he has worked for so long to hide. There was something about women — women like Reba, who would seize upon those hurts and try to mend the broken places and repair the damage and eliminate the scars — something instinctive in them that called out to them to try to banish pain.

The thought that suddenly occurred to him angered him still further. But he knew, in some deep place within him, that it was true. He began to realise that it was only the unwounded who failed to recognise wounds in the others with whom they came into contact. Reba knew his basic impulses were humane. His confessional, although made lightly, had proved that to her. As a result, she had been attracted to the Shannon who had once argued with his superior officer and then acted independently, flouting rules and ruining his career. And she had said she loved him!

Starson too had sensed the invisible scar tissue he bore that made him wage war when no call to arms had sounded. Starson, himself among the wounded, had only tried in his offcentre way to offer ... The word came, and Shannon tried to hurl it from his mind. The word: *love*.

Was love, then, in some strange way, his enemy? An image of the plastoid mother surrogate that had nurtured him floated in the air before him, all tubes and technocratic efficiency. He realised for the first time how hard he had tried to love that machine. The orderlies in the male compound where he grew up had been kind and helpful — even loving — in a brusque sort of way. But not one of them had he ever been able to call father.

The enemy was here in the cabin with him and would never surrender. The enemy would appear, he now knew, if he would but get up and look in the mirror on the wall. Starson and Reba were trying to vanquish that enemy. But he could not let them. Couldn't those fools see that? Couldn't they realise that they would kill him if they didn't stay away from the battle he wanted to go on waging alone?

The words that were crackling and sputtering from the communication terminal on his desk at last penetrated his consciousness.

'Oxon Kaedler,' a crewman was saying, 'has requested establishment of transmission. He wants to talk to you, sir. He says that if transmission is refused, he will destroy our ship. The crew requests orders. Over.'

Now, here, Shannon exulted, is an enemy with whom I will willingly do battle! Oxon Kaedler, who wants to buy my body and my business and who wants, as well, shadowy services from Reba Charlo.

He barked his orders into the communication terminal. 'I'll switch on the interchannel here in my cabin and talk to Kaedler. Tell the crew to tune in and stand by.'

The interchannel screen blazed into life, and the flame within it was Oxon Kaedler's image. He was being tossed above his air-vented platform — turning, turning. Grinning. Beside the mechanism stood the neomorph, and it was through the mouth of that creature that Kaedler's words came to Shannon as he stood waiting in front of the screen.

'Greetings, Shannon. And tidings of great joy. I have decided to be generous and repeat my proposition to you and your lovely lady. No, wait. Don't say anything yet. Let me once again outline my terms. Half a million Tokens for a single cell from your body. Half a million for a partnership in your business.'

Shannon said, 'There's obviously been an arithmetical error, Kaedler.'

'An error?'

'Your original offer, as I recall it, was a million Tokens for me and a million for the partnership.'

'My clerks evidently keep sloppy records. Fie on them! A million it is for each, then. I am not a quibbler.'

'Two million for each.'

'No!' Kaedler bounced in fury upon his air columns.

'No it is then,' Shannon remarked, enjoying the game.

When Kaedler's agitation visibly lessened, he said, 'Let me show you alternatives in the event that you refuse my offer this second and final time.'

'The screen diffused and then brightened again. At first Shannon was not sure what he was seeing. But then he recognised the outside of Kaedler's ship. He saw the nuclearods speckling its hull. The picture on the screen enlarged, and Shannon saw that the nuclearods were aimed at his own ship. He guessed that Kaedler had established a fieldfix between the two ships. Well, he had his own nuclearods. But the thought brought no comfort, because Kaedler's armoury was clearly more than three times the size of his own. Kaedler could maintain the fieldfix indefinitely, if he so chose. But he couldn't so choose, Shannon knew. He would open fire.

'I'll make a bargain with you, Kaedler. But not under duress. I'm headed for the Epicureanite Hostel. We can meet there. I don't want my crew endangered. After all, your interest is only in me and Reba Charlo.'

'True,' Kaedler agreed. 'But I won't meet you there. You must decide now. Don't you realise that the strength of my position derives in part from the fact that I can destroy not only you and Charlo but your entire crew as well?'

'Give me ten minutes — time to talk to Reba.'

'What quaint tricks might you and she not conceive in that small space of time to defeat me?' Kaedler's smile was broad as his words slid past the neomorph's lips. 'Ah, but no matter. They will fail, I assure you. So take your ten minutes. Talk to Charlo. Tell her my offer is still open — for ten minutes more. I urge you to be persuasive, Shannon. With Charlo and with yourself.'

Shannon switched the interscreen to 'Hold' and flicked a

switch on the communication terminal. He turned up the volume so that his voice would be heard at every crew station throughout the ship. He told his men that he thought there was a slim chance that they might be able to make a run for it but that Kaedler would probably be expecting them to do just that. He said he had a plan that might work — and might not. He would agree to board Kaedler's ship with Reba, but when the docking of the two ships was almost completed, they could fire their nuclearods and then immediately accelerate and make a run for it while Kaedler's crew was busy trying to repair the locks. But, he added, he would not attempt to execute his plan if the crew did not approve of it, since their lives would be risked as well as his own. He asked for a vote.

To his surprise, there was no dissent and almost no hesitation. Starson summed up the feelings of the crew following the affirmative vote in favor of attempted escape when he said, 'We signed on for the duration. We take the risks with the rations. We've already unhooded and nuclearods.'

Shannon drew a harsh breath and let it out before ordering Starson to bring Reba to his cabin.

When she appeared beside Starson a few minutes later, Shannon briefed her quickly on what was happening and on what he proposed to do about it. 'The crew is willing to attempt an escape. Are you?'

'If I'm not? . . .'

'I'll revise the plan slightly. We'll get you safely aboard Kaedler's ship before making a run for it.'

'Do you think you can make it?'

'We just might.'

'If I board Kaedler's ship . . .' Reba hesitated.

Shannon waited for her to go on.

'I couldn't stay with Kaedler.'

'He could arrange for reestablishment of your Legal status.'

'But when I left him — and I know I would leave him — he'd have it rescinded again. It seems there are few options open to me.'

Starson stepped forward. 'Excuse me, Shannon, do you mind?'

Shannon looked at his watch.

'Reba,' Starson said softly, 'opt for Kaedler. For safety.'

She put her arms around him and leaned her head against his shoulder. 'When we were both younger, Starson, we thought that nothing could harm us because we were together. I believed then that we'd always be together. I always felt so safe with you. Now you are here again, and so am I, and we are talking about safety as if no time at all had passed. But it has, and we have changed. We've learned that there's no safety anywhere. At best, we can only obtain a semblance of safety while we love. If Kaedler destroys this ship, I won't survive. But if I go with Kaedler, I know I will not survive there either — at least, not in any way that still matters to me. So I'm going to stay here.'

Shannon cut off Starson's protests by ordering him to take Reba down to the cargo hold where she would have a greater degree of protection from any attack that might be forthcoming. When they had both gone, he turned on the interscreen again and told Kaedler that he and Reba would accept his offer in exchange for a guarantee of safety for the ship and its crew. They were to be allowed to leave as soon as the transfer was completed. Kaedler readily agreed to the terms Shannon outlined, reminding him that he had no interest in either the crew or the ship — only in Shannon himself and, of course, Reba.

Shannon watched the docking maneuvers from the command cabin. When the lock corridor began to ease out from Kaedler's ship towards his own, he ordered the firing of the nuclearods. He watched the threads of white light spurt out and eat into the body of the approaching ship. Most of the blasts had been concentrated on the lock corridor and had shrivelled it. Shannon hoped that there had been penetration of the sensitive lock valves.

'Accelerate!' he shouted. 'Increase thrust capacity to maximum!'

The ship nosed upwards and to the left. The crewmen performed their tasks as swiftly as possible under the felt force of the increased velocity. The ship gradually reversed course, unable now to continue on to its destination, since Kaedler knew that destination and would undoubtedly pursue them in time.

'Bring Reba up from the cargo hold,' Shannon told Starson, as he continued to stare tensely at Kaedler's ship on the screen. 'Lock her in her cabin.'

'Shannon,' Starson said, his face tight and his voice rasping, 'there's no need to —'

'Alter course!' Shannon suddenly shouted in alarm. He quickly outlined coordinates and degree data.

Starson, startled, looked up at the screen and saw the deadly drones that Kaedler had launched. As they neared the ship, they surpassed Kaedler's own ship in size, seeming to fill the screen.

'It's no use, Shannon,' Starson said, all anger gone now from his face and voice. 'They're homing on us as a result of Kaedler's fieldfix.'

'Fire!' Shannon commanded.

But the blasts of deadly light from the nuclearods were deflected by the oncoming drones.

Less than fifteen seconds later, the first drone hit the ship. And then so did all the others.

The crippled ship shuddered violently under their impact, and the indicators recorded seriously reduced thrust. Shannon ordered the activation of the emergency filtration system and the automatic sealing off of major portions of the ship. He ordered Starson to check the astromaps at once in the hope of finding a safe setdown site.

'Only two planets offer possibilities,' Starson reported a few minutes later. 'Survey teams list them as U20 and U21. Both are unexplored.'

Shannon took the astromap from Starson. 'Activate the atmospheric shield. Try to make U20. It's closer.'

At that moment, the screen above the damaged control panel glowed faintly, and Shannon looked up to see Kaedler's image appear in flickering, fragmented lines.

'Before completely destroying you, Shannon, there is one last rather ironic item.' Kaedler's voice sounded shrill as a result of the damage done by the drones to the electronic system of the ship. Kaedler gestured to the neomorph, and the creature obediently held up a piece of paper.

Shannon recognised the formula for the Mythmadness pellets written on it. 'How . . . ?'

'Some time ago, I traced the men you employed in your manufacturing process,' Kaedler gloated. 'I paid them well and then put the pieces of their knowledge together, and now I shall inherit the mantle of the Mythmaster!'

'I should have known,' Shannon barked. 'You never intended to set up a partnership.' He braced himself against the control panel as his ship heaved about him.

'There is no need now for me to buy it, true. But I would still have considered a partnership, Shannon. You could have been useful to me. I would have enjoyed life in your body. But now those possibilities no longer exist — not for you, not for Charlo.'

Shannon threw a steel slide rule at the screen, and it cracked and spluttered into silence. He looked through the viewplates as Planet U2o came into view, and then strapped himself into a cradle. He became aware of a faint yellow haze, which, as they bore down and entered the planet's atmosphere, turned into a brassy glitter unlike any sun he had ever seen. He flicked switches on the control panel and pressed buttons, some of which did not respond, just as if this were another routine landing.

And then the gilded glow of the planet exploded into an ebony cloud that was totally encompassing.

CHAPTER FOURTEEN

From somewhere in the sooted world in which Shannon drifted came a sound. And then, at last, light.

The light came and went, white hooves fracturing the blackness. The hooves gradually became geometric warriors routing the night. As his eyes opened all the way and fought to focus, day dawned upon him and on the metallic chaos that had once been his ship.

Through the shattered viewplates, he saw a bronze sky and heavily foliated trees that sloped at absurd angles. It took him some time to realise that it was his ship that sloped, and not the trees.

The sound came again, and he wondered what it might have to do with him. He managed at last to crawl on his hands and knees to answer the urgent sound in which his name now and then lay imprisoned.

He crawled past the ruptured body lying over the bent stanchions, unwilling to look at the face it bore and which might mouth unspeakable indictments. He passed more bodies sprawled in the thoughtless postures of death.

He eased himself down the ladder to the lower deck and on to the cargo hold, where he found Starson dazedly bending over Reba's limp body. He seemed to be trying to protect her from further depredations.

'She's alive,' Starson wheezed. His voice quivered with shock. 'But she's unconscious.'

'Hurt?'

'I can't tell. I don't think so. But she broke free of her cradle when we hit.'

Shannon examined Reba's body but could detect no broken bones. Her skin was cool and unmarred except for a bruise on her left temple. He knelt beside her as he fought the darkness that threatened to envelop him again.

Starson remained leaning weakly against the cargo hatch and rubbing his shoulder.

'Starson!' Reba had regained consciousness and was easing herself upon one elbow.

'Here,' Starson answered. 'I'm over here.'

She looked around slowly, and seeing him, held out her hand. He came over to her and slipped to his knees beside her.

'Easy,' Shannon whispered to her. 'Don't move. How do you feel?'

'Weak. Afraid.'

'We won't have any trouble breathing the atmosphere of this place,' Shannon commented, 'because the viewplates are broken and the lock has been ripped open. The planet's air is already inside the ship. We're breathing it.'

He suggested that they try to negotiate the ladder, one at a time. He would go first. Reba could come next. Then, Starson. That way they would be able to help her up. It took them some time, and once Reba nearly fell, despite the support Starson was providing from below. At last, they reached the lock.

'Starson,' Shannon muttered, 'help her out of here. I'm going to check on the crew.'

He waited until Starson had lowered himself to the ground and had helped Reba down. Then he made the rounds of the ship. He found only two of the crew still alive. Rawley was one of them. A steel plate had torn loose and sliced flesh from Rawley's arm. He had managed to stop the blood flow with an improvised tourniquet and makeshift bandages.

'There's morphine in the lab,' Rawley said. 'I'll get the medical supplies and do what I can for him.' He nodded in the direction of the injured crewman lying nearby.

When he returned, he wordlessly administered morphine, and with Shannon's help, applied a splint to the crewman's leg and bandages to his wounds.

'Sir,' the man said to Shannon. 'Do you think we can repair her enough to make liftoff?'

Shannon told him to take it easy, avoiding answering the question. He was pretty sure that the ship was beyond repairing, and he suspected that the crewman knew it too. 'I'm going out to have a look around. I'll be back. Hold on.' He went to the lock. 'Rawley, do you think you can make it?'

'I can make it.'

They made their way out of the lock and dropped to the ground.

An overpowering feeling of light headedness seized Shannon. He fell back against the side of the ship that was tilted at a sixty-degree angle and shook his head in an attempt to clear it. He felt almost giddy, and for a moment he suspected the effects of shock as the cause. But he knew his feeling was not caused by shock. Neither was it caused by loss of blood. Except for multiple bruises and certain clusters of muscles that screamed in protest whenever he moved, he was uninjured. He took a deep breath. His feeling that was almost euphoric increased. He took another breath, consciously tasting it. The planet's air was different from the air on Earth or in spacers. It probably had a higher oxygen content. That would account for the feeling he had, which was decidedly pleasant and tended to counteract to some degree the pain with which his body was still protesting recent events.

He took a step away from the ship, and then another, with Rawley moving beside him. They went to where Starson and Reba sat beneath a tree that was garlanded with creeping vines and heavy with a green, rubbery foliage. Shannon was surprised to find himself bounding across the ground despite the pain his movements caused. He tried to slow his pace, but he continued bouncing among the thick trunks of trees. Every step he took lifted him more than six inches off the ground. He covered the remaining distance more quickly than he would have thought possible.

'The gravity is relatively low here,' Starson said as he arrived. 'And the oxygen content of the air is pretty high.'

'What's the noise?' Reba asked, startled.

They listened. The sound that Reba had heard was a random but steady series of sharp clicks, with no discernible pattern. They couldn't distinguish its source. There were no animals visible in the trees overhead or in the thick undergrowth. Only the hot sun occupied the sky; no birds could be seen.

'It might be caused by the branches of the trees rubbing together,' Rawley ventured.

'We'd better conduct a brief reconnaisance mission,' Shannon said. 'Reba, stay here. If anything happens, yell. We won't go far.'

'I'll go with you,' Reba said. She struggled to her feet with Starson's help.

'You'd be better off staying here,' Shannon said.

'Let her come,' Starson said. 'There's no telling what dangers this place might contain. She'll be better off with us.'

Shannon moved away from them. 'Keep your steps short and your feet as close to the ground as possible, or we'll go bouncing off in all directions.'

They walked for less than twenty yards, struggling to keep themselves from spurting upwards into the lowest of the tree branches, before they came to clearing.

'Look!' Reba cried. 'It's like a garden of golden jewels!'

Shannon studied the carpet of gilt spread out before them. It was mounded throughout, and he estimated it as approximately one acre in size. Perhaps lumps of sap had fallen from the trees above. But most of these mounds were too far from any trees to support that hypothesis. They were almost perfectly rounded, he noticed, and they melded against one another on the soggy ground that was dampened by the steadily dripping moisture from the foliage overhead.

'Wait!' Starson called out as Shannon began to make his way towards the gold crust. 'You don't know what—'

'I'm going to find out.' Shannon bent down and tapped one of the globules with his knuckles. It was hard and unyielding. He stood up and beckoned to the others.

'That sound we heard is coming from this stuff.'

It was true. There was an unnerving clicking, as of muted castanets, coming from the crusted carpet at their feet.

Reba began to move away from the group.

Starson yelled to her to stop, and when she didn't, he set off in pursuit.

Shannon, cursing them both, hurried after them, leaving Rawley behind.

Reba stopped some distance away and pointed down into a valley and then across the valley to the mountain veering skyward almost a mile away.

Shannon stared at the mountain glinting in the sunlight. The valley below him was aglow. 'Whatever it is, it reflects light,' he observed. 'Maybe it's some kind of coral formation.'

'Whatever it is, it's beautiful,' Reba said. 'There's another patch over there at the base of the trees.'

Rawley joined them. 'It's alive,' he stated. 'Watch closely. You can see it move.'

They stared at the yellow mass and realised that Rawley was right. There was a barely discernible movement within the formation. It was visible mainly in a shifting pattern of reflected light as one or more of the units that made up the mass changed position slightly.

'The clicking,' Rawley commented, 'is probably caused by the grating of those mounds against each other.'

'The mounds,' Shannon observed, 'are about the only really solid thing around. The trees shed water. Even their bark is moist, I noticed. The planet is almost a marsh.'

' "Swamp" would be a better word,' Starson said with some bitterness. 'Or "bog." '

'Let's head back to the ship,' Shannon suggested. 'We've got to measure the extent of the damage and see what repairs, if any, can be made. Since this planet is charted but unexplored, there is little likelihood that any ships will set down here. We've either got to repair the ship and leave under our own power or prepare for an indefinite stay until an ecological evaluation ship arrives.'

'Which could take years,' Rawley said thoughtfully. 'Especially considering the fact that Garth's Galaxy has a low priority in the Ecosystems Bureau's schedule.'

Shannon began to limp back towards the dense growth of trees. The others followed him in silence. As they passed into the green world beneath the tree boughs, warm water dripped down upon them from the foliage.

They found walking difficult, because the ground sucked at their feet and occasionally oozed up around their ankles. They arrived at the clearing in which the ship had crashed, and began to move towards it.

'Starson,' Shannon said when they reached the ship, 'check out the systems. Rawley will help you. Reba, see if there's anything you can do for the crewman on main deck. I'm going to check the communications net.'

It took them less than an hour to discover what each of them had secretly suspected. The ship was unrepairable. The interscreen was a fused metallic mass of tubes, wires, and conduits. No pressure could be raised to activate the airlock's pneumatic seal system.

Shannon expressed the thoughts of all of them when he said, 'Kaedler's won. We'll never get off this planet unless a ship lands here and takes us off. In the meantime, we've got to establish survival conditions.'

'It could be a long meantime, Shannon,' Rawley remarked.

'It could. The sun's going down. We'll spend the night aboard the ship. In the morning, we can begin our preparations.

'There don't seem to be any animals or birds here,' Reba said. 'Or people.'

Rawley proceeded to make a bunk on the main deck beside Avery, the injured crewman, and prepared to bed down there. Reba went to her cabin and found it uninhabitable due to the wreckage strewn about it. Shannon decided that they had all better sleep on the main deck. As the sun slipped below the horizon, they lay down in the sudden darkness that abruptly ate the ship.

Shannon lay within it, listening to Avery's moans and the spaces of silence that bracketed them. He imagined he could hear Reba breathing at the far end of the deck. The ship seemed to hold them in its battered arms, unable any longer to protect them because of its own evident mortality. Someone turned over heavily, seeking the temporary surcease from struggle that was sleep. Outside the ship, no moon rose. Shannon found little comfort in the fact that they had survived the disaster Kaedler had inflicted upon them, because he was painfully aware of the potential for new disasters that lay ahead for them. The planet might yet be discovered to be inhabited by hostile life forms or forces – or both. He wondered what form they might take if they came. He wondered if they would come — ever. Or would the planet simply lay soggy and silent beneath their feet while they met each new day with the knowledge that death was no stranger to this or any other world?

Avery moaned again, a declaration of life and its companion, pain.

Shannon heard Rawley whisper something to Avery. He couldn't distinguish the words. The moaning stopped.

Shannon awoke, uncounted hours later, listening. Something had awakened him. What? Avery was silent. No one moved about in the darkness. And then he recognised the sound that had awakened him. It was the clicking sound of the yellow formations they had discovered and examined earlier. But the clicking was much louder now. Or was it nearer?

He threw off his blanket and got to his feet. With his arms outstretched and taking short, tentative steps in the thick darkness that flooded the ship, he made his way towards the open lock. When he finally reached it, he peered outside but could see nothing in the weak light of the distant stars. With no moon to light the night sky, nearly total darkness reigned, and within it, sound. The clicking became a kind of ghostly chittering. It seemed to come from everywhere. He strained to see, but the stars failed him.

Someone brushed up against him, and he started. 'Rawley?' he whispered.

'No, it's me.' Reba's voice was strained. 'That awful noise woke me.'

'Be careful. The edge of the lock is right here.'

He felt her touch him, a moth fumbling about, blind and sightless. Equally sightless, he reached for her, and she moved closer to him. 'I shouldn't have taken you on this trip,' he said after a long period of silence. 'I should have insisted you stay in Underdenver.'

'I wanted to come.'

The chittering that filled the night almost obliterated Reba's words. But Shannon had heard them, and they pleased him. He thought about how he had ordered her locked in her cabin after she had destroyed his cell shipment. Well, now the prisoner had burst her bonds and escaped into the larger prison that was this world designated Planet U20 on the astromaps. As Reba nestled against him, Shannon wondered if he were still, in any sense, her jailer. It was a task he wanted very much to abandon, but he was not sure he knew how to do so.

'Shannon?'

'Yes?'

'What do you think will happen to us?'

'I don't know.' He knew he should speak brave words and outline bold plans for their escape from the planet. But he also knew that his brave words would be lies, and his plans mere fantasies.

Reba shifted position and put her arm around his waist. 'Perhaps it's not so important. Perhaps the most important thing is what *has* happened to us. You know that something has happened — to you and me?'

'Yes, I know.'

'It's too late,' Reba whispered, 'to stop it happening. Do you want to try to stop it, Shannon?'

'As you say, it's too late to stop it.'

'That doesn't answer my question.'

'No, I wouldn't want to stop it.'

'Now you are truly vulnerable. But you needn't be afraid. I have never been your enemy.'

He put his arms around her and lowered his head. He found her lips and forgot for a time the moonless sky, the shattered ship, and the incessant chittering flowing out of the darkness that shrouded the planet and everything on it.

When they separated, it was Reba who spoke for both of them. 'Shall we go outside?'

'No, it might not be safe. We can go down to the lower deck.'

They made their way slowly along the corridor and down the ramp. They lay down together on the lower deck, unable to see each other, able only to touch and taste the rich messages that their subsequent union proclaimed.

Afterwards, Reba slept with her head resting on Shannon's chest. He remained awake, feeling her breath warm on his body and welcoming her slight weight, which, instead of burdening him, seemed to uplift and free him in a way he had never before known.

A sense of exhilaration possessed him, but it surrendered at last to the onslaught of sleep. When he awoke sometime later, he forgot for a moment where he was. Reba's body beside his own surprised him until he remembered what had taken place. Then he gently spoke her name, and she stirred. Faint light was flowing down the ramp. He realised that there was no longer any sound coming from outside the ship. 'Reba,' he whispered, 'it's morning.'

She murmured sleepily and reached out to touch him. Her fingers felt cool now; last night they had been torches that had set his body ablaze. He pressed her fingertips to his lips and sat up.

'Don't go yet,' she sighed.

'It's morning,' he repeated, yearning for the night that had ended.

'Everything is so quiet.'

'Let's go up to main deck.' He held out his hands. She took them, and he helped her to her feet.

They climbed the ramp together and went past the lock, catching a glimpse of the sun surmounting the mountains, and on to the area where they had begun the night.

'Where's Starson?' Reba asked, looking around the area, which was empty except for the unmoving form of Avery.

'He and Rawley are probably outside. I'll take a look.' Shannon headed back to the lock. Before he reached it, he heard his name being called and recognised Starson's voice. It had come from outside the ship. At the lock, he paused. Starson and Rawley were standing some distance from the ship and pointing towards it.

'Shannon!' Starson yelled again, gesturing. 'Come on out. Look!'

Shannon leaped to the ground and turned to look back at the ship. He barely suppressed an exclamation of surprise.

'They're all over it,' Starson said as he came up to Shannon. 'Rawley was the first one out a few minutes ago. He called me. The mounds must have ... have migrated or something during the night.'

Shannon, staring at the ship, shielded his eyes from the sunlight being reflected by the masses of mounds that covered the entire ship. There was no single piece of surface metal visible. The broken hull was a shimmering sea of golden light. The mounds obliterated it and flowed down to the ground and away from it in a thick, undefined line.

'They're climbing the trees,' Rawley declared.

Shannon and Starson joined him. He pointed to the mounds that covered the trunks of the trees and most of the lower branches. 'These things are on the move. That was why we heard them all night long. It looks to me as if they're either migrating, as Starson said, or else going through some stage of their life cycle.'

'They're changing colour, too,' Starson observed.

'You're right,' Shannon said. 'Look, Rawley. Those on the branches up there are darker in colour, almost orange. The ones lower down on the trunk are still yellow.' He paused and glanced back towards the ship. 'We'd better find a way of sealing the ship, or we'll soon have company inside.'

Rawley had moved to the nearest tree and was bending over a cluster of mounds that had become separated from the larger mass that was mounting the tree trunk. As Starson and Shannon watched, he stroked his chin thoughtfully and straightened. 'They seem to be pulsing — vibrating. There's a kind of movement within each individual mound. You can spot it if you look closely. And you can definitely feel it if you touch them.'

Shannon bent down and placed the palm of his hand over one of the mounds. 'They seem to inflate and then deflate slightly. Yesterday they were almost motionless.'

'It may be maturation,' Rawley commented. 'Or metamorphosis. It's hard to be sure with alien life forms.'

Reba's scream suddenly split the air and brought all three men to life. As if they were units of a single mechanism, they began to race back towards the ship.

Shannon reached it first, just as Reba prepared to leap down to the ground. He held up his arms, and she dropped into them.

'What's the matter?' he asked anxiously. 'What's wrong?'

Reba's face was drawn, and at first she could utter no words.

'Easy,' Shannon whispered, holding her and feeling her body shudder against his.

Starson and Rawley stood by helplessly, waiting for Reba to speak.

'The crewman . . .' She glanced up at the open lock. 'Shannon, we've got to get out of here!'

'Avery? What about Avery?'

'Those things!' Reba cried. 'They're in the ship! I was down in the galley, and when I came back up, I . . . They killed him! They *ate* him!' She began to sob, and thrust a fist against her mouth.

Shannon cautiously pulled himself up on to the main deck and disappeared within the ship. 'Starson!' he yelled a moment later.

When Starson had joined him, he pointed to the pile of bones strewn about the deck.

Starson gritted his teeth and said nothing.

'We shouldn't have left him,' Shannon muttered. 'He never had a chance.'

'The morphine immobilised him to some degree,' Rawley

said as he climbed on to the deck. 'We'd better get out of here, and fast. Those things out there are moving towards us!'

The mounds that were moving towards them had changed in colouration from a glittering yellow to a deep rubine.

The three men abandoned the ship. They found Reba standing where they had left her. She was staring at the grove of trees in the distance. 'Shannon,' she said. 'Look.' She pointed to the trees.

Shannon looked and saw the mass of rubine mounds that were advancing towards them, the grating clicks that accompanied their almost languorous movement loud in the air.

'Rawley!' Shannon called out. 'Get the guns from the ship.'

Rawley remained motionless.

'Rawley, *move!*'

Rawley merely shook his head slowly from side to side. 'I'm not going back in there with those things.'

'I'll go,' Starson volunteered. He unholstered his gun and sprinted towards the ship.

'Make it fast!' Shannon shouted after him. He took Reba's hand and began to lead her away from the ship and out of the path of the mounds that were approaching it and them.

They took up a position several hundred yards away and waited anxiously for Starson to rejoin them. After what seemed like an interminable time, he appeared in the lock and leaped from the ship.

'He's got the guns!' Shannon exclaimed.

'Look out!' Reba cried to him.

Starson looked up and saw the mounds dropping from the hull of the ship. He leaped over them nimbly and began to run to where the others were waiting for him.

CHAPTER FIFTEEN

'That took guts,' Rawley said. 'More guts than I've got.'

Shannon nodded his agreement. 'Let's move on. We've got to find someplace that's free of those things. They were dormant when we landed here. Maybe they'll return to that state. In the meantime, we've got to keep clear of them.'

They marched in single file though the dense growth of trees, Shannon in the lead. As the morning passed, they discovered that the mounds were everywhere. There were clusters of them that stretched for as much as an acre, while other, smaller patches covered no more than several feet in any one direction. Some were still yellow, others orange, still others had attained the blooded look that Rawley speculated meant that they had reached maturity. The sound of their movements dinned in the air. The group made many forced detours in their line of march in order to avoid the omnipresent mound masses. They began to realise that the mounds were not, as they had had at first thought, hunting them. The creatures had seemed to them at first to move rather erratically, but it soon became apparent that their movements had purpose. The defoliated trees they passed testified to that fact.

While they rested in a clearing at the base of a mountain, Rawley offered the opinion that the mounds were a vital link in the planet's ecosystem. 'With the defoliation of the trees,' he said, 'the sun has a chance to dry up the ground, since there are no more leaves able to shed water. The sun is hot enough to turn this place into a desert if left to do its work without the counter-balancing force of the water given off by the trees. I'd say that, in time, the land will dry out — long before the trees can grow new leaves. And during that time,

I'd guess that the mounds will either die or hibernate. Then, when the new foliage matures and is once more on the verge of turning the planet into a swamp, the cycle will begin again.'

'I wonder if we'll be here to see it,' Reba said softly.

Rawley, lost in the speculative maze of his hypothesis, failed to hear her remark. 'The mounds evidently live on the foliage, but as we've seen, they'll consume other kinds of organic material. Incidentally, I believe the foliage is edible. By humans, I mean. I tried it, and it has a rather rubbery but not objectionable taste. I'd guess it's got a pretty high mineral content. It's probably protein-rich too.'

'If your idea is correct,' Shannon began, 'then we may have a chance of avoiding contact with the mounds.'

'How?' Starson asked.

'If we can find a defoliated area of sufficient size, we can stay within it and be fairly certain that no mounds are going to invade it, since there will be no sustenance available to them within it. I'm going to climb up to the top of this mountain and take a look around. Maybe I can spot a place nearby which the mounds have already passed through.'

'I'll go with you,' Starson said.

'Rawley, you stay here with Reba,' Shannon ordered. 'If any of those mounds appear, blast them.'

'I think it would be better,' Rawley offered, 'for all of us to stick together. We'd have a better chance that way.'

Shannon failed to hide his annoyance. 'Reba's tired. There's no need for her to climb this mountain. We may have a lot more walking ahead of us before the day is over. If you're afraid, Starson will stay here with you.'

'Go,' Rawley responded angrily. 'I'll stay here.'

Shannon set off up the mountain with Starson a pace or two behind him. The sun was high in the sky, and the heat was oppressive. By the time they reached the summit, they were both sweating heavily. Starson removed his tunic and draped it over his shoulder

'Rawley's theory makes sense,' he said. 'Look at the vapour rising down there in the valley.'

'It could take weeks, maybe even months, to dehydrate the planet though,' Shannon mused. 'Meanwhile, the mounds are as much a threat to us as they are to the vegation.' He shielded his eyes with his hand and gazed down into the valley and then off to the left, where low ridges of hills rose towards the sky. 'Do you see any place that looks safe?'

'It's like trying to see through fog,' Starson replied. 'Take a look over there at the first of those hills. Do you see the one I mean?' He pointed at the nearest of the ridges that serrated the valley. 'When the vapour drifts in the wind, it looks like the trees are all bare over there.'

'You're right. We'll head for that ridge. It can't be more than two miles from the base of this mountain. I wish to hell I had a compass. But everything of value is back on the ship. You don't have one, do you?'

Starson searched through his pockets. He pulled out one hand and examined its contents. 'I haven't got a thing worth having — here. A few Tokens. Keys. My cashcard. Stuff.'

'What are you doing with those?'

'These? I don't know.' Starson stared at the two Myth-madness antidote capsules lying among the Tokens and other paraphernalia he had retrieved from his pocket. 'I manage to collect the damnedest things. I've even got an old telescript here from a guy I used to know back on Earth.'

'Let's head back down. We'll have to set up some kind of camp over on that ridge before the sun sets.' Shannon began to move down the muddy mountainside, his feet sinking into the spongy morass beneath them.

'Shannon, wait.'

Shannon halted and waited for Starson to join him.

Starson hesitated and then said, 'We may never get off this planet. You know that as well as I do. I'm not particularly concerned about myself anymore, but I am worried about Reba. We've got to see to it that she doesn't get hurt.'

'I assume you're talking about the mounds.'

'Yes. The physical danger. But I'm also talking about other kinds of hurt. Shannon, be easy with her. You've got to be — now.'

'I'll take care of Reba,' Shannon said.

When Starson spoke, the sadness in his voice contradicted the smile on his face. 'That's fine, Shannon. I mean it. That's really fine, and I'm glad. I know Reba. I know her better than you do, although that will probably change as time passes — and if we survive this place. She's not really all that strong, you know. I'm not talking about her physical condition. Let me put it this way. When we were married, I always had the feeling when I was with her that I had to walk softly and smile a lot. Reba was younger then, and she was just beginning to find out that life could be cruel — gratuitously cruel — and that people were often insensitive and sometimes wilfully destructive to other people. Reba has never really come to terms with the fact that roses have thorns. I loved her very much. And she loved me. We still love each other. Only later, when things changed for me, and Reba saw that someone she loved could be hurt in a way she didn't understand and for reasons neither of us understood — well, she set out to establish what she must have thought of as armour against the world. She ran from life by running into the arms of men, and getting paid for the running, and believing all the while that no one could ever touch her again. Of course, she was wrong. You proved her wrong. So now it's up to you. And you haven't got much to work with here. Only yourself.'

Shannon had listened to Starson's remarks with a feeling that was composed of equal parts of guilt, dismay, and an eagerness to return to Reba, who had just been reincarnated for him in a new image as a result of Starson's words. 'I've only myself,' he said thoughtfully. 'It's all any of us has in the end.'

'But it can be a very valuable currency,' Starson said. 'The trick is to learn to spend it wisely.'

'I confess that I thought my account was bankrupt.'

'Not quite correct. You thought you *wanted* that kind of emotional bankruptcy. It's no wonder Reba has come to love you. You and she are alike in that respect.' Starson hesitated, and then, as if compelled to continue, went on. 'About that night in Underdenver, Shannon. It was a mistake. Hope is sometimes a mistake. Especially for people like me. People like me are always looking into cracked mirrors, and the images we see are distorted. But it isn't all the fault of the mirrors. It's our fault too, because we desperately see what we want to see. In the mirror, Shannon, you were ... Oh, just another distorted image, let's say.'

'We all have our mirrors,' Shannon said. 'And we all see in them what we want to see in the way we want to — or must — see it.'

Starson nodded solemnly. He stepped around Shannon and started down the mountainside. Before he had gone more than a few steps, Shannon caught up with him and took his arm. They stared at each other for a moment in silence, face to face, and then Shannon reached out and firmly gripped Starson's other arm. 'I've traded in my mirror,' he said, with evident seriousness. 'I found out that it was badly warped and more than a little bit tarnished. Fear can do that to mirrors as well as to men.'

After a moment, he released Starson, and they headed down the mountainside together.

They had almost reached the base of the mountain when an alteration in the light attracted Shannon's attention. He thought at first that it was the mound creatures that had caused it, but none were visible. The shadow came again a moment later, and this time he looked skywards. He felt something leap within him, and then he was yelling Starson's name and pointing up at the ship circling overhead.

'Fire your gun!' Shannon commanded, unholstering his own. 'We've got to signal them!'

The blasts of light from the two guns and the deep growl that accompanied them brought Reba and Rawley running. Rawley, when he saw the ship, began to fire his own gun.

'They're still circling!' Shannon shouted. 'They must have seen us!'

Overhead, the ship cruised in shrinking circles as if reconnoitering the territory below. It was unidentifiable but didn't resemble any known Patrol design. They continued firing into the sky, and then the first of the pellets dropped down nearby.

'It's Kaedler!' Shannon roared. 'Those are Mythmadness pellets. Run!'

The pellets struck the ground, and despite the softness they encountered, they bounded several yards up into the air again as a result of the planet's low gravity. The black hail that was so familiar to Shannon continued, and soon the ominous mist that harboured the essence of Mythmadness seeped out and over the area.

They ran through the trees and out into a clearing, only to find themselves confronted with a mass of moving mound creatures. Shannon signalled, and they headed back towards the trees as the ship roared overhead and the pellets rained down upon them.

It was hopeless. Shannon knew it was hopeless as the mist swirled about him and he lost sight of Reba and the others. He held his breath, but he knew that he would have to breathe sooner or later.

When he could no longer stand the searing pain in his chest, he opened his mouth and drew in great gulps of air, and with them the insidious chemistry of Mythmadness.

A sudden shifting of patterns, a thieving.

The reality of Panet U2o gave way before Shannon's eyes, and the invisible thief that was now abroad in the land stole the known and comprehended, and, in pack-rat fashion, left in its place a menagerie of miracles born in the brains of those suddenly wonderstruck by the mystic touch of Mythmadmadness.

Shannon saw the trees bend and sway to form an alphabet whose letters spelled out obscenities.

He laughed at the sound of tinkling bells that he vaguely recalled having heard in an earlier dream and that were yellow and orange and red. And that moving, mounded out there in the obsidian and angular distance.

Musk from the leering nymphs in the glade nearby drifted past his nostrils, tantalising, teasing.

Trinkets and toys, he thought, as the figurines fell free of their studs in the sky and trickled down his forehead, into his eyes, prying open the corners of his mouth as they whispered the words they had learned by studying the evil alphabet of the trees.

'Reba,' he said to the toy perched on the tip of his nose. It smiled at him and then somersaulted out of sight. He pursued it and all the others tumbling down around him, and they grew larger and joined together, and he found himself holding a life-size, flesh-and-blood toy that clawed at him with her fingers and shouted something very odd about stellar offspring.

'Reba,' he said to her, wondering why she fought him. He let her go, and she went stumbling away from him without a backward glance or a good-bye. He turned away from her.

And then, 'Mother!' he cried out happily to the masked woman who suddenly materialised, rocking in her chair and smoothing her gingham gown. 'It's me!'

'*Bastard!*' she screamed at him.

'Yes, but —'

She vanished.

The trees concluded their lesson with a warning. Looping and bending, twirling their branches, and twisting their roots high above the ground, they spelled out: BASTARD.

He turned away as the trees smirked, satisfied.

Something . . .

He spun around.

Ah, there!

The man was slinking hooded through the trees that moved no more. Shannon stalked him. He had to see his face, learn his name, say, 'Hello, my name is John Shannon, I think; what's yours, you faceless father of mine?'

The man, seeing that he was pursued, began to run. So did Shannon. The man leaped aboard a glittering Ferris wheel, and the wheel began to turn, while Shannon stood helpless below, waiting for it to stop, ignoring the cries of all the other little boys who surrounded him and who wept because all the seats were filled with the same hooded figure, who munched popcorn and ate candied apples and tossed the empty boxes and the denuded sticks down among them.

And then Shannon was on the Ferris wheel, and the hooded man was down below pressing the button that turned it. The wheel began to whir, frightening the lights adorning it. Shannon held on tight. Every time he whizzed past the ground he pleaded with the man to stop, please stop, he had never meant the man harm. Not ever. But the man paid no attention, and the wheel spun faster and faster, until the lights all winked out and it tore loose from the girders supporting it and flew high up into the sky, still turning, and the stars were the only lights visible, all of them cold and silent and as unfathered as Shannon himself.

He felt himself falling, and he enjoyed the sensation. He sprouted the wings he had been holding in reserve for just such an occasion and flapped down to the ground and fell upon the unsuspecting man who was counting tickets that all bore the name 'John Shannon'. Shannon tore up the tickets and ripped the hood from the man's head . . .

Maxevitch!

Shannon recoiled.

'You want to fuck or fight?' Maxevitch challenged, raising a bloody fist and unzipping his trousers.

'Reba, where . . .?' Shannon heard himself moan.

'Don't change the subject!' Maxevitch barked. 'What's it going to be?'

'It's all the same to me,' Shannon said, resigned.

'Maybe that's your trouble' Maxevitch said. 'Why'd you kill me?'

'Didn't.'

'Did so.'

'That Starsonofabitch was wrong.'

Maxevitch shook his head. 'Nope. I'm dead. See.' He showed Shannon the skull where, a moment ago, his face had been. And then he was gone.

'*Fuck you!*' Shannon shouted after him, but he couldn't achieve an erection, and so he pretended to himself that he hadn't wanted one anyway.

148

The bells were chiming somewhere nearby again, their voices full of warped cymbals and the whining of whipped dogs. They moved slowly in their yellowness, in their orangeness, in their gleaming redness.

'How do you do?' Shannon said to the bells that were not bells but something he was sure he would remember, given sufficient time. They were nearly at his feet, and he backed away politely so as not to impede their musical progress.

There was someone coming.

'Starson?' Reba said.

'I have no family connections,' Shannon answered.

'I've looked everywhere,' she said, disappointed. 'You have to do that when someone you love is lost.'

'Yes,' he said. 'I guess maybe you do. What is your name?'

'Once you — someone — called me "Girl of Gomorrah". And "Citizen of Sodom". You don't remember.'

'Did you read the trees?'

'There are no trees here. Only palaces and kind kings. A little while ago, I saw a unicorn. It was white and had a lovely golden horn. No, there are no trees here. You must be mistaken. You and your friends.'

'I have no friends.'

'Oh, you have!' She pointed at the creatures moving nearby and grating noisily against one another. 'I can't understand a word they say. But then I was never any good — at languages.'

'Where are you going?'

'To find my unicorn.'

Shannon followed her, because he had to, since the rest of the world around him had, all at once, disappeared. She was a beacon and the only real thing in the surrounding nest of shadows.

They wandered for hours, sometimes speaking, sometimes silent, through groves of trees and across dry expanses of near-desert. Time was dead. Space was stillborn. Reba stooped now and then to pick up pieces of a quartzlike material which she said was her treasure fallen from its chest.

'Shannon!' she cried suddenly, halting. 'Oh, no, it isn't Shannon after all. It's my unicorn. See?'

Shannon saw the man standing on the slight rise in the land, but he could not see any unicorn. The man was bare-chested, as someone he knew had only recently been. The name came to him then quite clearly. *Starson.* Now who was . . . ?

Reba began moving towards Starson, who was standing quite still, staring up at the sky.

'Wait!' Shannon called after her. 'You'll break all the bells!'

'Music doesn't matter to me. And I really must go. Don't you understand? My unicorn is there.'

He caught up with her and roughly threw her to the ground. 'The bells!' he bellowed. 'You almost stepped on them.' He looked down at her and then at Starson in the distance. He noticed that Starson was surrounded by the oddly shaped bells that were singing as they moved towards him and the other man lying unmoving on the ground nearby.

Reba cried out, 'What are you doing?'

'Birds!' came Starson's answer. 'I'm freeing all the birds.'

Not birds, Shannon thought. They're . . . He concentrated. The word came to him suddenly. 'They're *Tokens!*' he yelled. 'Not birds!'

'Free!' Starson cried. 'All of them, free.' He continued tossing Tokens in the air. 'But they can't fly! They're just fledglings. Yes, that's it. Or is it that their wings are broken?'

Shannon took a backward step and slipped over a ridge and fell heavily against a tree trunk.

'Wake up!' Reba called down to him. 'Are you asleep?'

When he regained consciousness some minutes later, he got to his feet and scrambled up the ridge. Something in him had altered subtly. He had felt himself changing. He looked up into the sky. Kaedler's ship still circled there. He looked around for Reba. She was moving steadily towards the bells — no, towards the mound creatures that were advancing on Starson. As they moved they left behind a cluster of white bones. Shannon shook his head, sifting through the few fancies that still lurked there, and remembered having seen Rawley lying near Starson, *Rawley!* The things had eaten Rawley! 'Reba!' he roared. 'Stop!'

But she continued moving forward, her eyes on Starson.

He ran towards her, stumbling and trying to fully free his mind from something he could not name. He caught her just as she was about to step on to the moving mounds. 'No!' he growled as he seized her.

'But —'

'No!' He looked across at Starson, who was searching through his pockets. At the same moment, more pellets fell from Kaedler's ship.

Shannon felt himself succumbing once again to the mist of Mythmadness. He fought to maintain control of his mind, breathing shallowly. 'Starson!' When Starson turned, Shannon called out to him, 'Get out of there. The mounds! They'll kill you!'

Starson looked down at the mounds and then across at Shannon. He held up the two antidote capsules he had found in his pocket.

Shannon looked around frantically. There was no way to reach Starson without running the risk of being consumed by the mounds that had cut him off and were marching relentlessly towards him. 'The capsules!' Shannon yelled. 'Take one!'

Starson raised a hand to his mouth and then slowly lowered it. He looked at the capsules in his hand. And then at Shannon and Reba. 'I don't want . . .' he began. 'No. No more wanting for me.' He tossed the capsules to Shannon, who caught one and retrieved the other, which had fallen to the ground. He offered one to Reba, and when she refused to take it, he forced it into her mouth and held her jaws clamped tight until she swallowed it. Then he took the other one.

As the antidote began to take effect, he drew his gun and blasted a tree to the ground. He hauled it to the carpet of mound creatures and let it fall across them. 'Starson, cross over! Use the tree! Hurry, man!'

The mound creatures began to drag Starson down. His arms flailed wildly, and an agonised cry broke from his lips. *'Shannon, help me!'*

Shannon knew what he had to do. He raised his gun, aimed, and quickly fired. Starson crumpled. He fired a second time as the mass of creatures began to move over Starson's body.

Reba turned on him and fought him furiously, in an attempt to break free of the grip he held her in, so that she could go to Starson.

When she realised her efforts were fruitless, she stared in silent horror at the moving mass until at last Starson's bones appeared in its deadly wake.

Only then did she scream. Hysterically. Over and over again.

CHAPTER SIXTEEN

When at last her screaming stopped, Reba began to whimper. She made soft, wet sounds and plucked idly at her lips and her hair as she sat on the ground beside Shannon. In the distance, the red mounds were barely discernible. Only small patches of them could be seen here and there. The air had cleared; no mist of Mythmadness now swirled anywhere.

'Reba,' Shannon said. She turned to him with a smile of infinite sweetness. 'Reba,' he repeated, 'are you all right now?'

'Of course. I'm fine.'

'I'm going to signal Kaedler's ship. It's our only chance to get out of here.'

'Do we have to leave?'

'Reba, do you remember Oxon Kaedler?'

'Oxon Kaedler? No, I don't believe I do. Should I? Is he a friend of yours?'

Shannon wanted to cry out or curse, but there was no one to cry out to and nothing to curse. He was both frightened and angry. The very sweetness of Reba's smile, the calm tone of her voice — these were the masks that her madness now wore. It was a madness that had nothing at all to do with the deadly rain that Kaedler had sent showering down upon them. This was something else, and worse. At the sight of Starson's bones left behind by the mound creatures to glisten wetly in the golden light of the sun, Reba had started to scream. Her cries had pierced the sky, rising and falling, and they had continued for more than an hour. She had dropped to her knees, bending over and wailing while she clawed at the ground. Shannon had tried to lift her up, but she refused to let him touch her. She had remained that way, while her screams grew weaker and the trembling of her body lessened. She had taken her head in her hands then and rocked mournfully back and forth. Eventually she had become silent.

Shannon had not understood her condition at first. She seemed to talk rationally enough. He told her that he had shot Starson to save him from the marauding mounds that had cut off his chances of escape. She mentioned the fact that she had swallowed one of the antidote capsules. She reminded Shannon that he had also taken one. Her accusation was plain, although only implicit in her statements. She was telling him that they had survived at the expense of Starson's life, and were, therefore, guilty of his death. She was suggesting that, had Starson kept one of the capsules, he might have saved himself. Shannon talked softly to her, saying that he didn't believe Starson wanted one of the capsules. Yes, it was true that he was Mythmad at the time. But, he reminded her, Starson had been about to take one of the capsules when he made his remark about 'no more wanting'. It was then that he had tossed the capsules to Shannon.

Reba admitted the truth of everything Shannon said. But, she pointed out, the tree Shannon had thrown as a bridge across the mound creatures could have been used by a traveller in either direction. Shannon, she suggested, could have run across it and dragged Starson back to safety. Shannon tried to explain to her that it was already too late by the time he had felled the tree. But he failed to convince either her or himself.

'Starson is dead,' he told her again as gently as he could. 'You've got to face that fact, Reba, and accept it, because it's true.'

She shook her head slowly from side to side. 'No, you're alive.'

It was then that he knew for certain. He caught a glimpse of something or someone ghosting across Reba's face and vanishing from her eyes. When the moment ended, he knew that a Reba other than the one he had known now stood before him. This one was secure in the irrational denial of terror and happy in an exclusive reality that would admit to no knowledge of death or pain.

'Beauty,' she was saying, 'like love, can never really die. Not as long as there are people who believe in it.' She touched Shannon's face and laughed gaily. 'You see, it's true. You're alive.'

'Do you know my name?'

'Oh,' she sighed airily. 'Names don't matter all that much. Mine was once Reba, I think. But now you must call me "Star". Will you?'

'I will.'

'Say it.'

'Star.'

She clapped her hands and leaned over and kissed his cheek. 'It sounds so lovely. I shall call you . . .' She hesitated. 'Your name must fit, mustn't it? It must define your power and your beauty, and it must most certainly encompass your kindliness. I shall call you . . . "King". Do you like the name?'

'Yes. I like it very much.'

'Now that we know each other's names, we're no longer strangers.'

Shannon took her in his arms, and she began to sing a soft, wordless song. She nestled against him, still crooning, as the sun began its daily descent. 'Wait here,' he said. 'I'll be gone only a minute or two.'

'You'll come back? You won't leave me alone?'

'I won't leave you.' He made his way to the top of the ridge that surmounted the clearing, and unholstered his gun. He looked up at Kaedler's ship and then quickly blasted several of the denuded trees standing needled against the sky. They burst into flames that shot quickly skywards.

When Kaedler's ship set down, Shannon knew, his defeat would be final. But it was the only thing he could do, the thing he must do. There was no way of knowing when a ship from the Ecosystems Bureau might visit this planet — if ever. He was prepared to submit to Kaedler, believing it to be the only way to save himself and Reba.

But surrender was to be denied him. Kaedler's ship, as if in perverse response to Shannon's desperate signal, was not setting down, but instead streaking across the darkening sky.

First the ship vanished. Then the sun disappeared.

Kaedler's departure, Shannon realised, was the bitter symbol of his total triumph. He could not have known who had survived the crash and the attacks of Mythmadness. But now he knew that someone had. The survivors, whoever they were, had defied him. Now he had defied them this one final time by ignoring their weak signal of need.

As he made his way back down the dark ridge, Shannon felt no hatred for Kaedler. He had not looked forward to submitting to him in order to ensure his — and Reba's — survival. Survival now was a matter he must manage. And he vowed that he would manage it — somehow. The mound creatures could be defeated. Now that he knew their pattern of behaviour, he could build defences against it. Fire would stop them. So would a barrier of metal that could be stripped from his stricken ship. A man could always find ways to defeat predators. And predators were every-where — in the worlds of all the galaxies as well as in the cities of Earth. His were here, and the battle that he had begun against them must continue. He remembered that Rawley had pronounced the foliage of the trees edible. The thought gave him some small comfort.

Reba welcomed him back with a warm embrace. 'Did you do that for me?' She pointed up at the still-blazing trees that stood like fiery totems on the ridge.

'Yes,' he lied. 'To light our way back to . . .' He had been about to say, 'to the ship'. 'To light our way home,' he said instead.

They walked through the gloom that was only faintly pierced by the light of the steel stars in the night sky, and came at last to the ship. Shannon asked Reba to wait outside for a moment. He climbed aboard the ship and found it deserted by the mound creatures. He took tools from the ship's locker, and for the next hour cleaned the interior of corpses and the bones of Avery, all of which he buried some distance from the ship, along with the remains of Starson and Rawley.

Reba watched his activities placidly. When the graves were completed, she stepped up to them and gently placed upon each of them pieces of quartz she had collected earlier.

They returned to the ship, and she prepared a meal, which they ate in the shattered galley. Afterwards, they lay down side by side on the main deck.

So our life together here, Shannon thought, as Reba moved closer to him, begins with the building of a graveyard. And I must continue to be, as I have been, a master of myth. In Reba's myths, I will now live so as not to betray the illusions she needs in order to survive and still love.

'King?'

'Yes, Reba?'

'Not "Reba". "Star".'

'Yes, Star?'

'Shall I tell you a story?'

'Tell me a story.'

'Once upon a time, there was a young king who was very unhappy. He came to visit me in a place far away from here, and he said he was unhappy because he had forgotten how

156

to love. I told him that I had also forgotten. But then, after we'd been together for a while, we both began to remember. And then we began to love again — each other.'

When Star finished her story, King put his arms around her and told her a story of a lonely world that had never before witnessed the miracle of human love. He told her it was that love which set the lonely world's sun afire each new day and made fruitful the ivory unicorns that inhabited the land.

Before he had finished his story, sleep claimed Star. King lay contentedly beside her, no longer so terribly alone, and glad of that fact — glad that he no longer felt compelled to insist that his destiny was a singular thing.

He thought about tomorrow and the days after that, and knew he would spend them with his eyes raised often to search the sky. Because someday a ship might come. But he was deeply afraid. Because he knew that none might ever come.

'King!' Star cried out, stirring in her sleep.

As he soothed her and she became quiet again, King found that his fear was diminishing. As he held Star close to him, his fear began to flee before the knowledge that he could now, at last, need and love and let himself be needed, be loved.

Also by Leo P. Kelley

THE MAN FROM MAYBE

The lost memory, the computerised harem of Superstud, the flight from the dreaded Marsman . . .

You lose your memory; and you find a new lifestyle.

You seem to lose sexuality; and you find a new type of lust.

You lose your sense of time; and you find time re-paced and re-defined.

You search for yourself; and you meet 'Helen of Troy' and 'Professor Apocalypse'.

You read this book; and you are taken into worlds that are frightening and unknown.

Leo P. Kelley

THE COINS OF MURPH

Toss the coin; toss the coin; toss the coin – and travel through Time with the aid of Chance.

Beforeit became Afterit and Afterit shall never be the same as Beforeit. For once Mankind made decisions; and Murph has ordered a change in the ways of man.

The wheels of Murph grind slowly, but exceedingly small; and Randland waits for the Losers. But once the Toss has been Lost and Murph's power has been questioned – then shall the need to voyage through Afterit become more important, and the power of the Coins be diminished.

A SELECTION FROM SOME OF CORONET'S LEADING SCI-FI WRITERS: